DATE DUE

Discoveries

Short Stories of the San Juans

by Kent Nelson

Western Reflections, Inc.
Ouray, Colorado

Library of Congress Catalog Number:

ISBN   1-890437-16-6   Hardcover
        1-890413-15-8   Softcover

Western Reflections, Inc.
P.O. Box 710
Ouray, CO 81427

1998
First Edition

Cover art, cover and interior design by Marti Ottinger

ACKNOWLEDGEMENTS

These stories originally appeared in slightly different form in the following magazines:

"Discoveries" in *The Southern Review*; "One Turned Wild" in *Cimarron Review*; "The Actress" in *Mid-American Review* (winner of the Sherwood Anderson Prize); "The Spirits of Animals" in *Denver Quarterly*; "On the Way to California" in *The Iowa Review*; "A Way of Dying" in *Context South*; "Wind Shift" in *The Sewanee Review*; "Encounters" in *Epoch*; "Light and Rain" in *Southwest Review*; "Perfect Stranger" in *Southern Humanities Review*; and "Toward the Sun" in *The Missouri Review*.

ii

DEDICATION

For Charles Wrye and Linda Wright-Minter

Other books by Kent Nelson

The Tennis Player and Other Stories
Cold Wind River
All Around Me Peaceful
Language in the Blood
The Middle of Nowhere (stories)

Contents

Discoveries

A rliss, as usual, did not watch the scenery. She sat on the far
side of the front seat writing in her journal while Jack drove
the two-lane toward Cortez. The desert was yellow and orange,
hot, sunbleached. To the north were the museum pieces of
Monument Valley, but Arliss didn't pay any attention. Jack tried
needling her by veering across the center stripe and sliding the car
dangerously close to the edge of the pavement above an arroyo,
but Arliss remained unfazed. She looked up now and then, obviously thinking of something else, and then returned to her scrib-
bling, teeth grabbing at her upper lip.

They were going fishing in Colorado — or at least he was
— and it pleased him to think of the stonefly hatch on the
Animas. Tucson was behind them. Other troubles, like cash flow
or his stepson Nick or the hastily-done rendering at the office,
paled in comparison to trout fishing. But these other things were
still mixed into his reverie. He would have to do the drawings
over when he got back. He wished solving Nick were so easy.

He loved Nick, and not just because he came in the deal
with Arliss. He was a bright child, polite most of the time, and
more curious than other children Jack knew. At twelve he studied
far better than Jack ever had. He was pretty in a girlish way —
long, curly blond hair, like Arliss's, and dark eyes. The boy had
never warmed to him, though. Nothing broke the ice. "Don't try

so hard," Arliss said. "Let him come to you."

Jack had taken him skiing at the Arizona Snowbowl, helped him with his homework, kicked the soccer ball with him in the backyard. He'd have brought him fishing, too, if Nick hadn't had to go to his father's.

He wanted to teach Nick how to fish. Jack was not the greatest fisherman, anymore than he was a great skier, but he was proficient enough to enjoy the frustrations. He didn't mind the snags or getting cold and wet, or losing a few big ones. He had discipline: that's what he'd told Nick about soccer. "You practice," he said. "That's how you learn to do anything."

"Unless you're doing it wrong," Nick said.

In Cortez they stopped for gas at a new plastic Texaco. Jack ran his credit card through, then leaned against the butt of the Jeep and filled the tank while Arliss went inside to use the bathroom. He watched her long fluid stride as she moved away, the purse slung over her shoulder. Her jeans were tight, and she wore a loose red-and-white striped shirt, too bright for fishing. She looked like a Red Devil lure his father used for bass in Minnesota. He and his father had fished a lot together before his father had started drinking so much. The drinking had changed everything, and his mother had ended up married to that bastard Eddie Loesser, or Eddie Loser, as Jack called him.

Jack smiled at the idea of a trout's snapping at Arliss. She looked good to him, too, certainly the best woman he'd ever known. He reached in through the window and honked the horn at her. He waved, but apparently she was perturbed at him because she didn't return the gesture.

So what if he wanted to fish for a few days? Next time they'd go where she wanted. And anyway, he'd agreed if they spent two nights on the Animas, he'd drive over to Ouray and sit in the hot springs pool. That was a compromise, wasn't it?

The pump snapped off, and he got his receipt and got back into the driver's seat. Cortez was a town dominated by heat and trying to revise its slow history. He could live there as easily as Tucson, and it would be a good place for Nick — test the elements, learn about Hispanic culture, be self-sufficient. But there was no college, and not much of a library. What would Arliss be like without teaching?

He folded out the map. They'd followed 160 North to Shiprock and then to Cortez. One option was to continue on to Durango — that was a little east and south of where they wanted to go. The other choice was Colorado 146 to Dolores over Lizard Head Pass. What a name: Lizard Head Pass. That took them a little west, but the map showed a four-wheel-drive road through Ophir and over to Silverton.

He put the map above the visor on Arliss's side, then noticed her journal on the dash. Arliss's mind, if not her eyes, was open, always moving. She recorded everything. Once she'd read him her description of the Salton Sea, where they'd gone a year ago. The humid heat and the stench of dead fish and the dead trees in the water had made her feel as if she were in the anteroom of death.

Jack had thought that silly, but he'd said nothing. She could feel however she wanted to. But to him, to see all those orange groves and date palms, to imagine a new huge lake had been created there in the '20s where there had been none before — that had been exhilarating.

He picked up her journal and opened it to see whether he could find what she'd written about their excursion to the Chiricahua Mountains. They'd camped out in Cave Creek Canyon and looked for some odd bird — a trogon — that Nick had heard about. The pages had only a few dates on them, and he skimmed a line or two here and there to get the chronology. She had tiny, meticulous handwriting. Of course he was familiar with it, but even he couldn't make out certain words. 'Very' looked like 'wavy,' and some words had to be deciphered by context. Jack teased her that she wrote in code.

He paused and read a random paragraph to see whether he should page forward or back.

> I imagine RG's doing to me what Jack does, can
> even sense his skin against mine, the touch of his
> finger. Would he if I asked him? Could I ask?

Jack glanced up and saw Arliss inside the Texaco buying a Diet Coke. Her red-and-white blouse wavered through the glass. She smiled at something the attendant said, a brilliant smile. Then she breezed out the door.

Jack snapped the journal closed and put it back on the dash. Heat was already in his face. She moved through the sunlight swinging her purse as if nothing had happened.

He pretended to delve in the glove compartment, and when she opened the door on her side, he looked up to the visor. "Oh, here it is," he said. He pulled the map down and leaned away into the driver's seat.

"That man in there was funny," Arliss said.

Jack unfolded the map again over the steering wheel and started the engine. Ahead of him the asphalt was a steaming black sheet, and he gunned the Jeep into the street. As soon as they'd swerved onto the highway, he felt her gaze.

"What's wrong with you?" she asked.

"Nothing."

"What is it this time?"

"Look at the clouds," he said. "If it's raining on the Animas, I'll be pissed." He stopped at a light, took a few deep breaths to calm himself, and looked at the map. "Let's take Lizard Head Pass and the four-wheel road across at Ophir," he said. The light changed and he handed her the map. "What did the man say that was so funny?"

All the way to Dolores, Arliss was content to drink her Diet Coke and stare out the window. When he could see her eyes, her gaze seemed to range beyond the road, beyond the river running alongside, and the cliff faces farther up. Or was he imagining? What did she really see? Who was RG?

He ran through a mental list of the people they knew — his friends first, the couples they socialized with, her friends at the university. He couldn't remember the names of all the professors and grad students, but it could be someone else, some stranger she'd met at lunch or on the bus coming home. *Would he if I asked?* Jack wondered whether she had.

He couldn't admit he'd read the journal, or he'd have confronted her right then. Once, when she was deciding whether to marry him, she'd asked whether he would ever read her mail. "Certainly not," he'd said. Privacy was the foundation of a relationship. Even if you shared a life, you needed space of your own.

"To grow in," she'd said.

"Yes, to grow in."

He liked the idea of her not knowing everything about him. He'd never told her how frightened he was at work when he submitted his drawings, or how lonely he'd been before he met her.

The road climbed on slow curves. The clouds had moved farther down, or they'd got closer. It wasn't raining yet where they were, but it looked as if it were raining in the mountains.

"I'm sorry about the fishing," Arliss said.

He was surprised by her voice. How could she even speak to him, knowing what she knew? But her tone was natural, even kind.

"I can't control the weather," he said.

The road climbed more steeply, and the mist of clouds oozed from the heavy timber beside the road. Jack leaned in close to the windshield to watch for the headlights of oncoming cars. He was all concentration. Why should she be silent? That was absurd. She didn't know he'd read anything, and anyway, what did the words mean to her? That was the important thing. She'd probably been in a mood several months ago and had forgotten by now what she'd written.

Frost had killed the grass, and aspen leaves were yellow draped in an eerie gray. What else had she written? Was what he read the account of a fantasy? A dream? If it were a dream, when had she dreamed it? He braked suddenly when the red brake lights of a truck loomed up from the mist.

Toward the top of the pass — he thought it was the top because the road leveled out — the trees diminished. It was raining now, hard steady rain. He followed the truck's lights around a bend. The journal was still on the dash. Black cover, maroon binding. She usually kept it in her purse which she carried everywhere. He wished she'd taken it with her into the bathroom at the Texaco.

On the downslope of Lizard Head Pass it began to sleet, but the driving was easier because they'd come out of the clouds. Jack geared down for the grade and used the brake sparingly. They wound along the flank of the mountain. The truck was still ahead of him. Lower down, when the sleet turned to rain, visibility was better, so he passed. To the northwest, the clouds were a lighter gray, etched with sunlight.

"I thought before we'd try the four-wheel road through Ophir," he said, "but we can't do it in this weather."

"Then what?"

"Maybe we should go to Ouray first. We can spend the night there while the weather clears."

"I thought you wanted to get on the river."

He shrugged. "It'll be too muddy."

He knew Arliss would trust his knowledge. He doubted this little bit of rain would make the river muddy. The tributary streams might rise, but at this time of the year the water would stay clear.

It was true he looked forward to time on the river. He liked the deep pools and the reflections of the sky and the rhythm of the water. Bubbles popped on the surface where the current moved over rocks, and insects were suspended like tiny helicopters over the eddies. He thought of fishing as pure time.

But it would not be pure time now.

They had last made love Wednesday night, two nights before. She was willing, and he lasted a long time for her pleasure. Afterward, they held each other before she'd drifted into sleep. She twitched, and he smiled at her childish expression illuminated by light from the street. But had she been lying all that time? Had she been thinking of someone else?

She claimed she was honest. "Jack, I've never told you a lie. Why do you lie to me?"

"What do you mean, lie to you?"

"I can feel it."

He had lied to her a few times, but they were small lies, like about money lost at cards or that the river would be muddy. Or they were innocent lies, like the time he had a few beers with Hank Carey, whom Arliss hated. Why get her started on that? Maybe he'd flirted a few times with women on the street — was that not-telling her a lie? He'd never lied about loving her.

Everyone had fantasies. He sometimes imagined making love

with Arliss's friend Kathleen, and he had reveries about Kim Basinger and Angela Bassett. Everyone had such ideas, especially about Kathleen. He smiled at that. He dreamed, too, and couldn't help his dreams. Sometimes there was another woman, and he'd feel the pleasure and moan.

Arliss woke him once in a fury. "What were you doing?" she asked.

"I wasn't doing anything. I'm right here in bed with you."

If he'd thought about it, he'd have assumed Arliss had such notions, too. She probably dreamed of Robert De Niro and William Hurt. But there was a difference between thinking something and writing it down. Thoughts were harmless spirits — ethereal, transient, and essentially meaningless. Words were solid. Words had intent and the drift of truth.

2.

The Placer View Motel in Ouray was within walking distance of the hot springs pool. When they were unloading the Jeep, the clouds had already broken up in the south, and the new sun slanted down over the cliff with a knife-like light.

"I don't understand why you want to stop," Arliss said. "I thought fishing was all that mattered."

"What do you care if I change my mind?" He lifted the backpacks from the cargo, carried them inside, and came back for the suitcase.

"I'd rather have my time of peace at the end of the trip," she said.

"We have to be flexible," he said.

The room was all right — large and sterile, with gold-painted lamps beside the bed and pastel green walls. A strained silence spread around them after Arliss closed the door.

Jack lay on the bed and watched her unpack her travel case. Then he got up. "I think I'll take a shower," he said.

He went into the bathroom, closed the door, and undressed. He felt no better in the shower. The hot water billowed steam into the small space, but the slag on his skin would not melt. He turned the water to cold and let the dross harden.

So maybe he was not the best lover of all time, but he tried to make her feel something. He wasn't the hump-and-run type. And she didn't complain. "You know me," was the way she complimented him. He thought that meant he did something right.

He turned off the water and dried himself briskly. He was clean, but not clean.

He emerged from the bathroom with the steam, a towel around his waist.

"How was it?" Arliss asked. She was lying on the bed, still in her jeans and red-and-white striped shirt, writing in her journal.

"Wonderful. You should try it."

"Since we're here, I'm going to the pool."

"Now?" He pulled the towel from his waist. "I thought we'd sleep awhile."

He lay down naked beside her and peeked casually at what she was writing. All he saw was the word 'never' before she tilted the journal away.

"Why can't I read it?"

"Because you can't."

"That's not an answer." He settled his wet head on her shoulder and touched the swell of her shirt.

"It's only four o'clock," she said, taking his hand away and putting it on his bare hip. She rolled up to sitting. "I'm getting dressed for the pool."

Never. The extreme case. Was it something he never did? Never said? Not ever? He told her he loved her often enough, perhaps too often. Was it something he never felt?

She stood and peeled down her jeans. Who else had seen this little act? She turned her back to him and pulled her shirt from the bottom up over her head. Then looking at herself in the mirror, she tied her hair up.

She was beautiful with her hair up, he thought. She had a long delicate neck, and wisps of blond fell across her skin. Her eyes seemed larger in proportion to the rest of her face.

"What are you watching?" she asked.

"You."

Did she go to motel rooms like this one or to an apartment somewhere? Her class schedule gave her lots of free hours. Did she meet her lover at an arranged hour, or whenever she could get away? In an office?

"I take it you don't want to swim," she said.

She slipped off her underwear, and he studied the flare of her hips, the drawn waist, the curve of her spine as she bent over the suitcase. She could have been a dancer as easily as an assistant professor of English. Her body was lithe, her movements graceful as a crane's.

She put on her suit — a one-piece with red flowers — and tied the top behind her back. He'd never thought about the suit before. It was revealing enough. When he'd believed she was unreceptive to stares, he'd not minded that other men admired her.

She picked up her journal and put it on the bureau. Then she slid a loose summer dress over her swimsuit.

"I guess I'll go," he said. "I wouldn't sleep without you."

The huge gray cirque above town was in bright sunshine. Pockets of snow still lay in the crevasses. The meadow high up was green against the blue sky. Too steep for skiing. Too steep even to climb, though someone must have done it. He thought of taking Nick climbing. No, Nick didn't like skiing; he wouldn't like climbing, either.

Jack had been to Ouray once before, in winter. Everyone wore parkas and boots. The hot springs steamed like a geyser pool. But now, as they walked down the hill toward the park, only a thin ribbon of vapor rose above the vine-covered fence. They walked apart on the path, Arliss's purse between them like a ticking bomb.

Or was the journal there? He hadn't seen her put it in her purse. She'd put it on the bureau — that's where he'd seen it last.

The frightening part was that she acted the same. Believing he was blind, she treated him as she always did. But what else was she thinking? She might stay with him a few weeks — months, maybe, for Nick's sake — but caring for him less and less. If she were honest, wouldn't she tell him if there were something to know? Would she tell him she was sick if she knew she'd get well? One thing was certain: he was not blind now.

Arliss paused outside the pool entrance and searched in her purse for her wallet. Jack didn't see the journal.

"Maybe I'll walk around town," Jack said.

"This is what we stopped for," Arliss said. "I'll pay, if you want."

"It isn't that."

"Oh, come on, Jack."

She got out her wallet, and he saw the journal sticking out from a side pocket.

There was one big pool divided into separate sections — a deep end, a lap pool, a cold-water game area, a three-foot warm water pool, and a hot pool. Jack stood on the apron and watched the swimmers doing laps. Some of them slid through the water so effortlessly, as if on oil, while others churned and splashed. He wondered whether practice really helped: would the thrashers ever become smooth?

Arliss came up behind him and gave him a push. "Watch out!"

He recoiled from the edge, and she caught him.

"Jesus," he said.

"Will you watch my things?" she said. "I didn't have a quarter for the locker." She pointed to the bench where her jeans and the Red Devil shirt were folded neatly across her purse.

She sat in profile at the edge, her shoulders hunched forward, weight on her hands, and tested the water in the hot pool. "It's hot," she said.

"You're not in any hurry," he said.

Gradually she acclimated. She slid further in, further, until she was waist-deep. "It's so hot," she said. She leaned against the side and immersed herself slowly until he saw only her face and neck. She closed her eyes.

He sat on the bench thinking of a pretext to look in her purse. If they'd been on a longer trip, he might have asked her whether she had her address book so he could write a postcard. Money. He'd brought his own wallet, plenty there. He glanced again toward Arliss whose eyes were still closed.

He jostled the jeans and shirt away from the top of her purse. It wasn't zipped all the way closed, but he couldn't see into it, either. He looked around to check whether anyone else was watching him. The game crowd was mostly teenagers and adults acting like children. A few smaller kids played under the leaking mushroom. The people in the hot pool were oblivious: either talking or stunned by the heat. He unzipped the flap a little. Gum, he thought. He was looking for a stick of gum.

The journal was there, tucked down along the side. He felt its sturdy back against the leather. Maybe he could steal it, and she'd think she'd left it somewhere, misplaced it. She was always losing her keys. Or he could take her purse and her jeans and shirt to the men's room. Safekeeping.

He picked up the purse and the clothes just as Arliss opened her eyes.

"Where are you going?"

"The men's room."

"I'll watch my stuff," she said. "Go ahead."

Jack had to put them down again. He walked to the men's room, though he didn't have to go. What he really wanted was a drink.

He smiled grimly. The odd thing was that at the same time he was miserable not knowing the truth, he realized a perverse pleasure in what had happened. For the last three hours, Arliss had taken on an intense aura of mystery.

He loitered in the men's dressing room, then came back to the bench. Arliss had moved to the other side of the pool facing him. When she saw him there, she waved. He didn't want to know more, but he had to. Yet, if he read the journal, he'd have to tell her, wouldn't he? Or would he only have to tell her if he changed, if he could not conceal his knowledge?

Arliss had her eyes closed again and was smiling. Was she luxuriating in the hot water or dreaming of RG? Or maybe their friend Ed Heitmann, whom she'd always liked?

On impulse, he pulled the journal from her purse. He couldn't help himself. He had no plan except to read as much as he could before she caught him. If it made a difference to her (he knew it would), they could have it out right there, in front of the people in the pool.

He leafed through the pages toward the back to find out what she'd written last. Never *what?*

He glanced up once, but Arliss's eyes were still closed. *Driving through the mountains on the way to fishing. Jack's uneasy, silent, closing me out. Or am I closing him out? I'd rather stay home than go on these excursions. He wants so much his own way. He's selfish and brittle and weak. Maybe what D says is true: he'll never be different.*

Same day. We have a motel room! Jack is sweet, but there must be a reason. He never does anything without a plan. Maybe he wants to look up some woman he knows here. I can't and won't think of that when I have my own....

He could not make out the next word. The writing went further down the page, but he looked up into the sun, confused and ashamed and angry. Arliss's expression in the hot water was blissful.

He put the journal back and closed the purse. He piled the clothes back on top of it.

He sat a minute longer with his eyes closed, face into the glare. He felt no warmth, but rather perceived sunlight shining through his eyelids like slivers of ice. Reds and oranges danced in the interior darkness, and he felt dizzy. Even on his bare arms, goosebumps prickled, and he rubbed his skin hard to get warm.

Arliss spoke to him, and he opened his eyes. He hadn't heard what she said.

He stood up. "I'm going to get a newspaper," he said. "Can you watch your own things?"

That night they lay in curved arcs, Arliss behind him under the covers. She rubbed his back lightly, but he didn't respond. *Selfish and brittle and weak.* Selfish maybe, yes. He wanted to go fishing and skiing, and he argued, and sometimes went over her objections. But she was invited to go; he didn't prefer to go without her. He wasn't deceptive. And there were many times he did what she wanted. He went to poetry readings or to movies with Meryl Streep in them. He went to her department parties, but she refused to go to his office picnics. Wasn't that selfish in the same way?

Brittle and weak: were those the same? Brittle as a dry twig, or as a pane of glass? A twig snapped; a pane of glass shattered. He did get hurt easily; he admitted that. When someone promised to call and didn't, or when he was left off a party list, he was let down. He took it personally when Jim Curry didn't like a rendering. He was brittle maybe, but not weak. How could she call him weak? His father had been a drunk, and his stepfather had beaten him, and despite all that, he had worked his way through college and architecture school. How was that weak? Sometimes he brooded about his job because the pay was low. And they had moved from one apartment to another because he never felt at home. But he had persevered with Nick. And he loved her. Was loving her weak?

D was her friend Diane, but they also knew two Davids. Which of them would say he would never change? Never? And there was Dob Milligan, who lived in Aurora, who quoted Colette and Laurence Durrell, writers Arliss liked.

Arliss tapped his back.

"What?" he asked.

"Why don't you want to make love to me now when you wanted to before?"

He didn't answer, and she slid her hand around his hip.

He couldn't bring himself to turn toward her. The desire he'd felt — certainly the teasing and the warmth — had left him, and her ministrations did not bring the usual urge. She had lied, if not in words, then in omission. He couldn't make love to her. And yet if he didn't, she'd write about that, too. God knew what she'd write about that.

He wanted to tell her he knew no other women in Ouray. Where had she got that notion? From Nick? Last winter at breakfast one morning, he and Nick had run into the wife of a friend who was out of town. But that had been coincidence. Could Nick have said something about that to Arliss?

He turned over finally and put his arms around her and kissed her, but his mind went spinning into other questions and vague answers and more questions until he had lost the thread of what he had meant to think of, which was what Arliss felt now. She saw through his ruse of holding her. He couldn't stir her passion or his own, simply by putting his body against hers. He kissed her further, across her neck and her breasts, and slid his hand along the flare of her hip.

But she went cold.

"Now what?" he asked. "I thought you wanted to."

"Don't."

He paused, kissed her again on the neck.

"I want to talk," she said, and pushed him away. She groped for the lamp beside the bed.

"Don't turn on the light," he said.

She didn't, and he lay on his side, fearful of what was next. How many journals did she have? He couldn't remember — six or seven, a hundred? He imagined page after page, thousands of pages documenting every tiny episode of their lives together, every argument, every reaction, every loud word, every nuance of emotion. He would always be the unfeeling one, the guilty one, the perpetrator. That was the pernicious part: she could make him over in any way she wanted to, as if her version of him were immutable and correct. How did he defend himself against that?

Arliss got up in the dark and went to the bathroom. He stared at the white outline around the door. The toilet flushed; water came on in the sink. He softened his heart and his opinion. The journals might be mere effusions, impatience boiled over rather than indictment. She needed an outlet. What was the harm in that? She could write what she wished to and did not have to measure the truth. Probably she didn't read them once they'd been written, and so against whom did he have to defend himself? It was cheap therapy.

But didn't what she write seem truthful to her? Why would she put down such words if they didn't reflect her feelings? And once she'd written them, the words had their effect on what she felt from then on. Density and mass altered inertia. A deer's tracks told where the deer had been and when and the direction it was going. Or was the journal more like an owl's wingprint in the snow?

She opened the bathroom door, but didn't turn off the light, and the shadow cast by her naked body moved across him like the moon's eclipsing earth. She came over to the bed. He turned away.

"Jack, you have to tell me what's wrong." Her voice was gentle. She sat down on the bed beside him. "Please." She pulled at his arm.

He turned slowly on his own initiative and gazed at her, the tears rising slowly in him, a spring seeping to the surface. "I don't know," he said.

3.

The Animas River came out of the mountains above and around Silverton and flowed down the canyon toward Durango. The railroad ran alongside the river most of the way — the canyon was the only place for the railroad to go. Jack and Arliss boarded the train in Silverton — a tourist run on a coal-burning steam locomotive that stopped in the canyon to let out backpackers and fishermen. Jack had always wanted to fish the parts of the river that were hard to reach.

They got off at the trailhead for Chicago Basin and unloaded their packs. His pack was heavy — most of the food and cooking gear, plus his waders. They had a choice to cross the footbridge here and scramble through downed timber and brush along the far bank or follow the train track. The train track was easier walking for Arliss, and quicker. It was better to keep morale high early on.

The Animas was fast through the canyon, and that morning not blue from the reflection of the sky the way Jack had pictured it, but rather green and golden brown from the aspens and birches along the bank, and black from the shadow of the cliff. When it plunged over rocks and fallen logs, the water was ruffled like lace.

Jack had seen some good pools from the train, and a creek coming in from No Name Basin, but he wondered what pools might be good farther down, too, where the train was now. He was looking for big fish, and peace — but he knew already there would be no peace.

The night before had been a nightmare. He hadn't told Arliss what was wrong, though she begged him, and then she'd become intransigent, too. He was to blame for her anger; he accepted that. Her bitterness for his silence had nowhere to resound, which made her more resentful still, and all he could think of was her writing furiously in her tiny script how he'd become devious and artful.

But was she so blameless as she made out? And was it sickness to want to know a truth which would hurt him? He'd lain in bed after Arliss had gone to sleep, and he remembered the day his mother had taken him into the backyard one afternoon in Minneapolis and had held his hand so tightly it hurt. "Your father's gone," she said.

"Gone where? When's he coming back?"

"Never," she said.

His mother had held him close, and he cried, and afterwards he had assumed, because his father had died so suddenly, he'd been sick in a way he was not able to comprehend. He was never able to attach a name to the sickness until his stepfather had moved in. Eddie Loser had beaten him, and his mother, too, and one night during a rage, he'd heard through his bedroom wall Eddie Loser say, "Is that what you want me to do, too, Gail? Kill myself?"

When Jack was old enough, he'd gone to the police. There were photographs of his father's old Pontiac parked on a country road, with the piece of malleable plastic hose attached from the exhaust pipe and run through the back window. But there was no picture of his father.

Arliss breathed slowly in sleep, and he'd got up, careful not to wake her. He'd sat by the window watching the traffic moving ghostlike along the highway. An electric transformer hummed nearby, and above him a half moon drifted above the sparse clouds. It would have been beautiful, he thought, if they had been out in the canyon.

"How far do you want to go?" Arliss asked. She'd been quiet for a good mile along the train track.

"Till I see the right place," he said.

"How will you know the right place?"

"I don't know."

"What was the moon last night?"

"The moon?"

"Doesn't the moon have to do with how the fish bite? You sat up so late I thought maybe you'd seen the moon."

"It was half."

He wished there were better fishing in the creeks. He wanted to get away from everyone, up into No Name Basin where no one went, where there was probably not even a trail except for game paths. He wanted to fish high, where he could see out across the mountains. His doubts would seem inconsequential. It was ludicrous to worry whether Arliss loved him or not. What did it matter if her love were imperfect? No thoughts or feelings were ever pure. Love was replete with inconsistencies, vagaries of lust and fantasy and the desire for free rein. No one had ever loved purely and completely another human being.

And yet he aspired to that pure love. He wanted her with him. He wanted to love her without thinking of her friend Kathleen or of Angela Bassett. He wanted Arliss to believe he was strong.

Or did he only care about not being deceived?

He stopped opposite where the creek fed into the river.

"You're going to fish here?" she asked.

"Trout feed where the creek comes in," he said.

He slid his pack off and sat in the grass beside the train track. The sun had just cleared the rim of the canyon and flowed through the trees on the ridge. The smell of wet grass was heavy on the air. Arliss did not look at the sunlight; she was watching him.

He unlashed the fly rod from the frame of his pack, slid the rod out, and fit the sections together. The rest of his gear — flies, leaders, assorted implements for repairs — was already arranged in his fishing vest which he unpacked from the stuff bag of his down sleeping bag. He unzipped the side pocket of his pack and pulled out the bone-handled knife.

Arliss hadn't moved even to take off her pack.

"You don't want to try?" he asked. He threaded the green flyline through the eyelets of the rod. "I brought you a spinning rod, all ready to go."

"No, thanks. What if I caught one?"

"You'd have to land it or let it go."

"I'll just read," she said. "Or write a little."

He stopped at the last eyelet and looked at her closely. An eerie sensation, sudden as the snap of a bone, made him shake.

"Write what?"

"Maybe a story. I don't know. Are we going to have lunch here, too?"

He was still trembling when he pulled the line taut to the reel. What did she mean 'a story'? A life story? A piece of fiction? She hadn't made up stories lying on the bed in the motel or riding in the car. He'd tried to recall the exact words he'd read, but couldn't remember the phrasing. His name was in it: that was real.

He pulled on the waders and fastened them over his shoulders, then tucked his arms into his vest.

"You go ahead if you're ready," she said. "I'm going to eat something."

"I'll leave the pack by that tree," he said. He pointed to a big spruce on a knoll above the river.

He carried the pack over to the tree. The river was thirty feet below. It curled around the knoll and under a rock on the far side. Too deep to cross there. They'd taken the railroad track for morale, but now he'd have to wade the river if he was going to fish back to this side.

"Will my purse be safe here?" she asked.

"Who's going to steal it?" Jack asked. "There's no one around."

She put her purse into the pack, then took a book from it. The journal was there, too. He saw it as she pulled out bread and ham, a packet of mayonnaise, and several miniature Milky Way bars. "You want a sandwich?" she asked.

"It's only ten o'clock," he said. "I want to fish."

"I'm not stopping you."

Oh, he loved her all right, but what did that matter if she didn't love him? He watched the way her eyes moved when she put together her sandwich, the ambiance of her mouth. She knew he was watching her. He felt at that moment he could kill her — she seemed so much in control.

"You want any chocolate?" she asked.

From the rim of the knoll there was a game path at an angle down to the river. The canyon leveled here where the creek came in just above the knoll on the other side. There were willows there and young cottonwoods along the rocky wash. About a quarter-mile upstream, the river bent left around a grove of cottonwoods.

Arliss sat on a shaded rock on the knoll, eating her sandwich. He wasn't sure where to fish — here, where she could watch and criticize, where the good pools were, or around the bend where she couldn't see him. There were rocky shallows here, free of background brush, and he cast a few times with a nymph to see what happened, to limber his arm and get the feel of the rod. It was maybe too open, too sunny for good fishing, too late already, but he didn't care. He wasn't thinking about the fishing.

Arliss finished her sandwich and climbed off the rock and down the embankment. At the edge of the river was a big rock in the sun; she was heading there. He rolled the line into an eddy, followed it into the run where the creek fed in. He pulled it and snapped another cast up into the current. He worked his way along the shallows in this way, pretending to fish up and across the current.

Arliss climbed the rock, found a niche and laid out her jacket, then sat down with her book. She tilted her face into the sun a moment, then looked up the river toward him. He followed the fly into the riffles of white water. Arliss opened her book.

Jack reeled and stepped back onto the rocks along the bar. The cottonwoods made a good shadow across the river, and the pool at the bend in the river was deep and slow, but he couldn't concentrate now. He walked into the trees where Arliss couldn't see him and leaned his rod against a tree. He took off his vest and threw it down. He walked through the trees and up the slope to the railroad tracks.

Then he ran. The waders were heavy and awkward and hot, but he didn't stop. The knoll was farther than he'd thought. The track bowed toward the steeper hill. He was going back for his knife. That was what he'd tell Arliss.

Would he laugh at himself? Was he foolish to think she'd been unfaithful? And what if she had been? Would he forgive her? That was a terrible thought: how much pain would forgiveness require? He would think of betrayal all the time, day and night, and wonder whether it would happen again. She would know he was thinking of it, that he knew. And her knowing he knew —

wouldn't that change everything, too?

Sweat poured from under his arms, down his legs inside the airless waders. He ran down off the train track and across the sage meadow to the knoll. The journal was in the pack in her purse, right where she'd left it.

He got the bone-handled knife first and put it in his pocket. Then he picked up the journal and carried it to the rock where Arliss had eaten her sandwich. The sun had moved higher, and now the river was sunlit. In the riffles downstream was a brilliant flash without color or depth, as if the light had its source not in the sun, but in the river itself. He was in no hurry. He sat on the rock, holding the journal in his lap, knowing he could not read it, but knowing he had to. He ran his hand along the hard spine of the book and closed his eyes.

He didn't hear Arliss until she was right beside him. "Jack, what are you doing?" she asked.

He opened his eyes. The sun was sharp against her smooth cheek.

"I thought you were fishing," she said.

The river was unmoving, hot light. He wanted to throw the journal into that whiteness, to have it explode like a star. But there were other journals, he knew, other evidence he'd feel compelled to discover, more things he did not want to know. He lifted his hand, and without its weight, the journal, the written-on pages expanded in the air. "You've come for this," he said.

He handed her the journal, and she took it. Then he got up and went to retrieve his fishing vest and his fly rod he had left upstream. ▲▲▲

One
Turned
Wild

It was six o'clock in the morning, and Marshall walked quietly
through the house not wanting to wake anyone. Only the dog,
Cindy, a rust and white springer, stirred. She followed him to the
back door, wagging her cut-off tail, and whined when he didn't
take her out with him into the cool morning.

Marshall walked out away from the house. He was a big
man, a little on the heavy side, and was dressed in dirty bluejeans
and a plaid shirt. He looked like a lumberjack gone over to power
saws: a hefty stomach, thick soft arms. He stretched his arms and
hands almost ten feet into the sky.

He loved the first moments of the day that seeped over the
garden and the wet meadow and the forest beyond. From his garden gate he saw pine and spruce all the way up to timberline, and
it seemed that morning he could walk up to the snowline as easily
as across the meadow. Whitehouse, Potosi, and Sneffels to the
south were already in the sun.

But he never had time to hike up to the snowline or go fishing or ride his ATV. All he managed was to get up earlier than his
wife and work for an hour in the garden before he went to work.
He stretched again to loosen his back, then went to the tool shed,
took down a hoe from its nail, and put a trowel in his back pocket. It was only a few steps to the garden, and he opened the gate
through the head-high woven-wire fence that kept out the deer.

He walked between two rows of strawberries, and about halfway down, a movement in the meadow made him stop. He looked up and saw an animal lying in the grass. By the color, he assumed it was a deer — dark cocoa — and it didn't move. Deer often grazed the meadow in the early mornings, but he rarely saw them lying down. Maybe it was sick.

Then the animal raised its head — a massive head with light eyes — and Marshall saw it was a dog. A big dog.

He watched it for a moment, and the dog watched him, too. It was larger than any retriever he'd ever seen. The dog rose onto its forelegs. He was thin, but strong at the shoulder, a Chesapeake Bay. He didn't look very friendly.

"Here, boy," Marshall called. "Are you lost?"

But the dog backed away and disappeared into the grass,

Marshall took the trowel from his pocket and kneeled down and weeded around each strawberry and runner. He didn't think about the dog; he thought about work — how he didn't want to go. It was Friday, a loose day anyway. But if he didn't go, it would look bad on his record. And the record mattered.

A half hour passed, and he smelled the bacon and eggs Miriam was cooking all the way out where he was. She rattled dishes and closed cupboards, too — her way of calling him inside. Needling. He'd get there, and the table would be set neatly, the spoons, plates, juice glasses. He didn't want to stop weeding.

The screen door opened with a wheeze, and Jeremy came out on the step. He was four, a sweet kid, dressed in blue overalls and a white pullover shirt, long brown hair already neatly combed. Marshall worried Miriam was making him a sissy.

"Daddy, Mummy says the breakfast is almost ready, and you're supposed to come in to clean up for work."

"Good morning," Marshall said.

"Morning, Daddy."

"Tell your mother I'll be right along."

Jeremy went back in, and the door banged closed, and Marshall knew Miriam would scold the boy for the noise.

The place they lived was worth the job, but Marshall hated the driving. It was seven miles on gravel road to the main highway, then another twenty to the department shed. From the shed, it was more miles to a repair site — sometimes he drove as many as three hundred miles a day. And he had to listen all that time to a motor — a car, a truck, a rock crusher, a jackhammer, a paver. He wanted quiet.

He stood up and took a last look at the meadow. The Chesapeake Bay was there again. The light had shifted enough or the dog had moved so its eyes glowed yellow. The eyes of a mountain lion, Marshall thought. Biggest dog he'd ever seen.

"How's the garden?" Miriam asked.

"Beans are sprouting. Lettuce is up. We should have some good strawberries."

"I don't like strawberries," Jeremy said.

"Well, you don't have to eat any," Miriam said.

Marshall walked to the bathroom and ran the water. "There's a big dog out in the meadow. Know who he belongs to?"

Miriam went to the window, and he waited for her voice before he washed his hands.

"I don't see anything," she said.

"Past the fence. Out in the grass."

"There's no dog out there," she said.

He walked to the window where she stood, towel in hand. He looked out, too, toward the grass. Nothing.

"Must have gone on home," he said. "Nice big dog. Looked like a Chesapeake Bay retriever."

He went into the bedroom and took down the clean overalls Miriam had hung neatly on a hanger. His shirt was folded and waiting on the dresser.

"You left your tools out there," Miriam said.

He put on the shirt and the clean overalls, but kept his dirty socks on. Then he went back to the kitchen and eased himself down in his chair. He took a piece of bacon from the plate in the middle of the table. Jeremy was already eating oatmeal.

"Wish I didn't have to go to work today," he said.

"You say that every day," Jeremy said.

"That's the way I feel everyday."

"You shouldn't say that," Miriam said. "You'll teach him work is wrong." She slid eggs from the skillet onto Marshall's plate, and then her own.

"I'm supposed to say I love driving a few hundred miles a day? I love the men I work with? They're so witty?" He looked at Jeremy. "Work's not wrong, son. It's just hard as nails."

"You're hard as nails," Jeremy said.

"The weekend's coming," Miriam said. "You can work on your garden all you want."

"I wish." Marshall forked eggs into his mouth.

"We do have to get groceries," Miriam said. "It's been two weeks. And you said you'd take Jeremy to the fair."

Marshall watched Jeremy spoon oatmeal into his mouth. "How about if I take you fishing instead?"

"The fair," Jeremy said.

"The fair only comes once a year," Miriam said.

"Fishing," Marshall said. "I don't want to go to the Goddamn fair. He hasn't caught a fish yet in his whole life."

"You don't have to swear," Miriam said.

"You don't have to swear, Daddy. We'll go fishing."

After breakfast, he shaved while Miriam fixed his lunch — two ham sandwiches with mayo cut into wedges. She put black olives in a cellophane bag, potato chips in a Tupperware container.

"Don't forget your tools," she said.

He finished shaving and put on his jacket, then went outside, more to look for the dog than to put his tools away. The sun was higher now — all the way down into the Blue Lakes Basin, and the morning rose in him like a spirit.

Maybe he'd move the family into Montrose where there were distractions like movies and miniature golf. He wouldn't have to drive so much. But the noise and dirt, the heat... That was the trouble: you couldn't live right in a city, and you couldn't get a decent job in the country.

The dog's eyes were on him. Marshall felt them before he saw the dog over by the tool shed twenty paces away. Its eyes burned yellow. They went right through him like no man's eyes ever could.

Marshall took a couple of steps toward the animal and held his hand out to give the dog his scent. "Here, baby," he said softly.

The dog's head was enormous, the skull a good ten inches

from ear to ear. Now that he was closer, Marshall saw its fur was matted and unkempt, and its haunches thin as a greyhound's. Marshall let the full force of the animal sweep through him.

He took a couple of steps closer, and the dog held its ground.

Marshall whistled low, raising the tone of his whistle at the end, and just when Marshall thought the dog might come to him, it raised up and backed away deliberately. Then it turned and crept soundlessly through the grass.

Marshall whistled again, but he knew the dog wouldn't come. No, sir, not this baby, he thought. This dog was wild.

"You're going to be late for work, " Miriam said.

He didn't look around at her, but collected the hoe and the trowel and put them in the shed.

In the kitchen, Marshall got out a pan.

"What are you going to do?" Miriam asked.

"I'm going to feed the dog."

"Did you look to see whose he is?"

"He isn't anybody's."

"What does that mean?"

"He's come out of the woods," Marshall said. "Go look at him. He's wild."

She went to the window and looked out, and Marshall watched her eyes for the recognition of what she saw. But she saw nothing.

"I think he must be a figment of your imagination," she said.

"Go out there to the meadow," he said. He rattled Cindy's food into the pan and ran water over it. Cindy came over, wagging her tail. "Not for you," Marshall said.

He went to the door.

"Wait, Daddy," Jeremy said. "I'm coming, too."

"No, honey, you stay here," Miriam said. "He's not a regular dog."

"I want to see him."

"He might hurt you, sweetheart."

"The dog isn't going to hurt anybody," Marshall said. "I'm going to leave the food at the edge of the yard."

He handed the pot of food to Jeremy, and Jeremy smiled. Cindy went to the door with them, wagging her tail.

"You stay here, Cindy," Miriam said. "At least you can do what I say."

Marshall and Jeremy went outside, and Miriam followed. They walked out past the tool shed and stopped and looked around. At first Marshall didn't see him — just the meadow grass waving in the breeze, the aspens beyond the meadow. A hawk circled along the perimeter. But then when he stepped forward, the dog crouched up from the grass.

"My God," Miriam said. "He's huge."

"A figment of my imagination, huh?" Marshall held up the food. "Here, boy. Come on now." Marshall put the food down. "He's probably been in the woods for a few weeks. Maybe some camper left him."

The dog looked at them with heavy yellow eyes.

"Here, doggie," Jeremy said.

"Here, boy," said Marshall.

"He's certainly not going to come," Miriam said.

Marshall looked at her. "You shut up," he said softly.

They glared at each other for a moment. Miriam's lip twitched, and then she turned, wordless, and took Jeremy's hand and went back to the house.

Marshall looked back at the dog. He knew the dog wouldn't come to him yet. If they fed him, though, he'd stay around, and they could tame him. That's what he hoped. It would take some time, but he was patient. Pretty patient. Sometimes he was patient.

He went back into the house.

"You're not going to go off with that dog out there," Miriam said.

"Why not?" Marshall said. "I've got to make a living." He liked his own sarcasm.

"You going to tame him, is that it?" Miriam said.

"For God's sake, Miriam. I just saw the dog."

"Dogs like that turn on you when you least expect it."

"All we have to do is win him over," Marshall said. "He'd be the most loyal dog you'd ever see."

"My uncle did that once. He befriended a dog somebody'd beaten. One day he raised his hand to scratch his head, and the dog attacked him."

"My head doesn't itch," Marshall said. He kneeled down to Jeremy. "You protect your mommy from that big dog outside. You hear me?"

"I will."

He gave Jeremy a hug and stood up. He turned to Miriam. "Let Cindy out later. Maybe she can lure the dog in."

"I'm not letting Cindy out," Miriam said coldly.

Marshall went to the den and took down his .22 and 30-30.

"What are you going to do with those?" she asked.

"Keep you from doing anything foolish," he said.

He took the rifles out with him to the truck.

At the maintenance shed he picked up his assignment for the day. Friday was usually light with the weekend coming behind them. He was scheduled to ride over with the supervisor, Jerry Mathias, to check on the grading up on Horsefly Mesa. Two guys to do one job: that was about right for the highway department.

Jerry was about his age, mustache, long hair. A good guy. And he drove.

"So what's the trouble?" Jerry asked him. "You get shut out last night?"

"Why do you think there's trouble?" Marshall asked.

"The way you look."

"How do I look?"

"Like there's trouble."

"Miriam," Marshall said. "She gets on my nerves."

"Like, my girlfriend doesn't get on mine?"

"I don't know," Marshall said. "Sometimes I think I should get out of here. Move to Montrose, maybe Durango."

"Everybody wants to leave where he's at," Jerry said. "But we don't do it."

Marshall looked out the side window, his sunburned arm tilted there. The country around them was high plains with aspen in the swales, and distance all around. The Elk Mountains were visible a hundred miles away over by Gunnison.

"Maybe we're lucky being so weak," Marshall said.

"You're dreaming," Jerry said. "Besides there aren't any jobs in town."

"For a man who'd work there's always something."

"What about the guns?" Jerry asked.

"The guns? Oh, yeah, the rifles. I forgot about them." Marshall picked up the 30-30 and ran his hand over the stock. "I brought them so Miriam wouldn't shoot the dog."

"What dog?"

"He came around this morning. Lean as a snake. On his own for awhile, I guess. A Chesapeake Bay retriever."

"So that's what you argued about?"

"Yeah, I guess. She's all scared, and I didn't want her to shoot the poor bastard."

"You got to be careful about dogs like that," Jerry said. "They got diseases."

"This one doesn't," Marshall said. "He has hunger."

They drove several miles in silence. Marshall had seen a lot of animals driving all those miles — thousands of deer and elk, a few bobcats, even black bears and mountain lions. But none of those animals intrigued him like this dog. Maybe he liked the dog for his hunger: the dog had done something — he'd escaped, hidden, lived free. Marshall envied that. He had hunger too, but for what? He didn't know for what. Maybe he had hunger for hunger. He wanted to do something. Something: that didn't say much. Do what? Something besides work.

Five-thirty and still light. Marshall drove his blue truck down the long gravel stretch toward his house. The sun angled from the Dallas Divide and shimmered over the gullies and ravines, the scrub oaks, the pines, the cottonwoods in the stream bottom. He turned at the driveway and surveyed the meadow. No movement. The air was still. He saw the house against the pines, the garden. Usually Jeremy came out into the yard when he drove in, but today the yard was empty. He parked out front and got out of the truck. No one to congratulate him for making it through another week.

Then Miriam appeared in the doorway. She had that hard-mouthed expression she got sometimes when she was angry.

"What is it?" he asked.

She began crying.

"Jesus, what?" Marshall thought of the cocoa retriever.

Jeremy ran outside, past Miriam. "Hello, Daddy," he said. "We're going fishing."

"In a minute," Marshall said. He knelt and put an arm around Jeremy. "Tell me what happened."

Miriam was still sobbing.

"The big dog ate Cindy," Jeremy said.

"What do you mean ate her?"

"Killed her," Miriam said. She stopped crying. "I let her out, like you said, and I watched through the window. The dog was eating from that pot, and he saw Cindy come over. He didn't move. He just let her come on, and when she was close enough, he turned on her."

"He must have thought she was after the food," Marshall said.

"It was terrible," Miriam said. "Thank God Jeremy didn't see it."

"Where's Cindy now?" Marshall asked.

"We've been afraid to go out," Miriam said.

He gave Miriam a pat on the back and went around the house to the back yard. He didn't see the dog by the shed where he'd put the food, or in the meadow. But he found Cindy. She was bloodied, her throat ripped, and her stomach eaten out.

Then the wild dog broke. He ran from the high grass behind the shed toward the meadow. He had a smooth, rippling gait and ran close to the ground, leaping effortlessly only once, to clear a log. He disappeared into the dark timber.

Marshall went back into the house and got a plastic bag from the cupboard.

"What are you going to do?" Miriam asked.

"I'm going to bury Cindy," he said.

"Is that all?"

"What else do you want me to do?" He paused and looked at Miriam. He knew what she wanted him to do. "I'm not going to shoot him," he said.

"Marshall..."

"Besides, I can't shoot him if he's not around."

He took the garbage bag outside and got the shovel from the shed.

The first thing he thought of the next morning was whether the dog had come back. The night before, after Miriam was in bed, he'd mixed hamburger with Cindy's cereal food and set it out by the garden. He got up early and dressed before Miriam turned over to find him gone, went quietly to the back door and looked out.

The sun hadn't cleared Pinnacle Ridge or Courthouse Mountain, though it shone on the top of the Sneffels Range. A low light hung over the meadow, and dew was heavy on the grass.

The pan was empty, but when he looked around, he didn't see the dog anywhere. He spent an hour and a half in the garden before Miriam called him for breakfast.

At the table Miriam was dressed in slacks and a clean print blouse. Jeremy had on his overalls and another clean shirt. She didn't mention the dog, but the idea of him was there like a scent.

"Are you coming with us to Montrose?" she asked.

"When are you going?"

"After we eat. I'm going to take Jeremy to the fair, and then I'll shop for groceries."

"I want you to go, Daddy," Jeremy said.

"I guess I'll go then," he said.

"You should," Miriam said.

The last judgment made him nearly change his mind, or argue, but instead he said, "He ate the food I put out last night."

"You put out more food?"

"Some hamburger," Marshall said.

There was a pause.

Marshall looked at Jeremy. "You're not afraid of the dog, are you, son?"

"No."

"Good."

"He killed Cindy," Miriam said. "You can't ignore that."

"I haven't ignored it," Marshall said.

"I want to pat the dog," Jeremy said.

Marshall smiled. "That's the spirit," he said. "So do I."

They spent the morning at the fair in Ridgway. Marshall rode the airplane and the whirl-a-gig with Jeremy, and they threw baseballs at bowling pins and ate hot dogs. Afterwards they drove to Montrose to the City Market. Marshall made an effort. He pushed the cart, didn't argue when Miriam bought the more expensive meat, the bouquet of flowers, the new toothbrushes. He wrote the check and wheeled the groceries out and loaded them into the back of the truck.

Then he drove back. The road from Montrose was clear, and Sneffels in the distance dominated the east-west ridge. Uncompahgre Peak and Wetterhorn lined the east side of the valley. It was just such mountains that made Marshall want to live where he lived.

They passed the pork-barrel dam at Ridgway State Park, and the highway turned southeast and went the longer way around the dam. Marshall had never thought of himself as an environmentalist, but he hated the reservoir's being there instead of the river. The water was drawn down three-quarters of the year, and the scenery was mudflats. Every time he passed it, he got angry.

That anger was still in him when he turned right off Highway 550 into Ridgway.

"I have to stop at Mountain Market," he said. "I forgot something at the store."

"What did you forget?"

He pulled left into the parking lot. "Beer," he said.

He jumped out of the truck before Jeremy unfastened his seat belt. "I want to come."

"I'll only be a minute."

He raced into the store. It was like every store he ever went into — confusing. A welter of colors, aisles, choices. He started in the vegetable section, but that wasn't where the dog food was, or the beer. Finally he asked a clerk stacking boxes of cereal on a shelf.

"I want Alpo," Marshall said. "Where is it?"

He brought a case to the check-out counter where Jason

Frank was open.

"Changing from the kibble, huh?" Jason asked. "You know, meat makes them shit like pigs."

"Just ring it up, Jason."

Marshall glanced at the door and saw Miriam carrying Jeremy into the store.

There was nowhere to hide, and it irritated him that's what his instinct was. Of course she'd see the dog food when he carried it out of the store, but it angered him she was coming to check on him.

"Where's the beer?" Miriam said.

"Beer's in the cooler on aisle 6," Jason Frank said.

"I was talking to Marshall."

"They only have 3.2," Marshall said. "And we needed this."

"I told him kibble," Jason Frank said.

"He has a wild dog he thinks he can tame," Miriam said. "It's a vicious animal."

Jason Frank looked at Marshall. "You have a wild dog?"

"I don't have him yet," Marshall said. "But I will."

"The dog ate Cindy," Jeremy said.

Jason Frank leaned over the counter. "Maybe you should call the sheriff in."

Marshall grabbed Jason by the white apron and yanked him close. "That dog isn't hurting anybody unless I teach him to, and I might in your instance. Now ring up the dog food."

He let Jason go, and Jason rang up the Alpo.

Then Marshall turned to Miriam. "And you don't help the cause."

It was four o'clock when they got home. The sun was still well up over Dallas Divide. Marshall unloaded the truck, and Miriam put the groceries away in the kitchen. Marshall carried in the case of dog food and took out two cans. "I'm going to put some out."

"Not now. Please. Can't you wait till it's dark when Jeremy's gone to bed?"

"I'm taking Jeremy fishing," Marshall said. "He'll be with me."

"I'm catching a fish," Jeremy said. "My first one."

Marshall opened both ends of a can and pushed the dog food through and into the pot. "It's good to conquer fear," he said. He smiled and opened the other can.

He and Jeremy took the pot outside and left it at the edge of the meadow. Then Marshall got his fly rod from the shed, and his fishing gear, and the little spinning rod he'd bought a month ago for Jeremy.

Jeremy was standing at the edge of the meadow when he came out of the shed.

"There's no dog," Jeremy said.

"There's a dog," Marshall said. "You just can't see him."

"It's a big place."

"Yes, it's a big place."

Marshall put on his vest and found a few worms under rocks near the garden. He put these loose in his creel. "Let's us men go fish," he said to Jeremy.

Miriam came out of the house. "Where will you be?" she asked.

"Down in the willows," Marshall said. "Not far." He felt sorry for her, worried like that. And it wasn't easy for her way out from town. He knew that. "You can come if you want," he said.

"I have too much to do."

"We won't stay down past seven."

"Be careful," she said.

They walked out of the yard and along the path to the creek. East Dallas Creek was not great fishing — small brookies — but it had a good flow of water out of Blue Lakes and Blaine Creek, and when the beavers built dams, the ponds could be okay.

Marshall set up Jeremy at a beaver pond with a worm on his hook.

"All you have to do is wait," Marshall said. "The fish will come to you."

"To the worm."

"That's what I meant. I'm going to be right over there at the next pond."

"You can see me."

Marshall waded the stream below where he'd settled Jeremy

and came up below another beaver dam to the east. He climbed halfway up the dam, balancing on sticks, and from there had a vantage point to cast into the pool. He didn't care if he caught anything. The point was to be out there.

He relaxed, letting the week's stress flow out of him through the flyline. He caught three nine-inchers and stowed them in his creel. Then Jeremy hooked one. Marshall heard him squeal. "What do I do?" Jeremy called.

"Reel him in."

Marshall waded back to Jeremy who by then had reeled the trout right to the end of the rod.

"A little one," Jeremy said.

"Six, seven-incher. Not so bad. Not to be ashamed of. You can show it to your mother."

Marshall took the trout off the hook and opened his creel. "We have enough," he said. "Shall we go home and eat them?"

"Can I carry my fish?" Jeremy asked.

"Sure you can."

Marshall threaded a stick through the gills and mouth and let Jeremy carry his fish. They climbed the bank and came down the path. The house was beautiful against the mountains. The soft light melted into the aspens and across the meadow. The sun still touched the tops of the peaks.

Miriam came out onto the porch and waved. She was a good wife, Marshall thought — caring, hard-working, a little too organized, but maybe he needed organizing.

"Can I show mommy the fish? Jeremy asked.

Marshall nodded, and Jeremy ran toward the house, holding the fish as high as he could in his hand. "Mommy, look what I caught!" His words filled the air.

He was halfway between them, almost to the shed, when the dog leaped from the high grass. Marshall had no time to shout. The dog made for Jeremy, though Jeremy didn't see him, and in three long strides was there. Jeremy didn't even cry out. He went down to his knees and the fish on the stick flew up into the air.

Marshall ran forward. "My God!"

❖ ❖ ❖

He was aware of Miriam's screaming at him, and he felt the pounding of her fists against his back.

"He's all right," Marshall shouted.

She did not stop her screaming and punching, and finally he turned and slapped her hard. "He's all right," I said.

She sat on the ground, stunned.

Jeremy was whimpering beside his father's leg. There was a little blood on his arm, a small trickle. Marshall pushed down the straps of his overalls and pulled off his shirt. He must have tripped and fallen just before the dog had got to him, and the dog had missed and had just caught the skin of his arm.

Then Marshall had got there, and the dog had run off.

It was standing a hundred yards away looking at them with its yellow eyes.

Marshall sat down with Jeremy, explaining to him about the dog, that the dog was wild and didn't know any better, but not to be afraid. Miriam got up and ran into the house.

They were still sitting there when Miriam came out carrying the 30-30. Her face was set very hard. She held the gun across her body. "You shoot that dog," she said. "Or I will."

They looked at each other for a long time. At last he nodded and took the rifle.

Jeremy got up and went to his mother's arms. Marshall stood there with the rifle.

"Shoot him," Miriam said.

Marshall walked a few steps toward the dog.

"Shoot!"

As she said the word again, the dog ran. He loped through the high grass, flew, it seemed, brown against green. Marshall lifted the rifle and got him in the scope. The muscles worked smoothly, legs bent, body low to the ground. He was beautiful, flying through the meadow.

Then Marshall squeezed the trigger, and the cocoa body crumpled and disappeared into the grass. ▲▲▲

The Actress

A ndrea's first reaction was annoyance: the red-bearded man would not leave her alone. He stood boot to shoe, his large red head tilted downward like a crested heron's, staring as if in contemplation of her avoidance. He was dressed in baggy blue corduroy trousers and a sun-yellow shirt, and his expression was impish as Huck Finn's, or maybe, she thought, it wasn't so impish after all. She searched the gate waiting area for someone to rescue her, but no one noticed the man's strange behavior except her. "All right," he said at last, "you can stay at my place." He smiled at the right moment to cancel hard feelings.

"I have reservations," Andrea said as tightly as she could.

"Hey, I'm talking about free rent." The man's face grew redder, and his beard quivered. He sat down beside her in the molded plastic chair. "Name's Miles Himmel," he said, holding out his wide hand. "I'm going to help you out."

Andrea, by some mystery, found her hand in his, grasped firmly by thick sweaty fingers. "I think I'm settled," she said. "Thanks anyway."

"Off to ski, huh? The one-week deal?"

"Ten days."

"From?"

"St. Louis."

The man inhaled. "A week isn't much time."

"Ten days," Andrea said. "No, it isn't much time, and I want to enjoy it."

"You've spent a bundle just getting to Denver, right? Then you have the package — supposedly clean condo, sauna, a hundred and forty bucks a night or more, bus service to the lift."

"Something like that."

"How many times have you wasted money on that bullshit?"

Andrea frowned. She did not like the way this man spoke, even when he was right. She had wasted money before — at the Tetons one summer, and last year at Sun Valley. She'd saved for months. "This is my vacation," she said, and turned away.

"Look, in Telluride, people are sleeping on the windowsills. My offer's genuine. At my place, there are no conditions, no hours, no responsibilities. You can ski down to the gondola station." He straightened up in his chair and combed his beard with his stubby fingers. "All true," he said. "I swear."

Andrea softened a little. If he were serious, it would be a blessing, of course. Perhaps she would even be more relaxed if she spent less money. But he was a stranger. One didn't trust strangers, especially red-headed strangers. "What did you say your name was?"

"Himmel," he said. "You have to take some risks in life, or otherwise you miss out." He paused. "Call your friends. We can stop at the police station, if you want. They'll vouch for me." He smiled and paused again. "One other thing — I won't bother you."

Driving the icy road down from the Telluride airport in Miles Himmel's Jeep seemed less crazy than the idea of it had while they were waiting for the commuter plane in the Denver airport. The lights of the small town tucked in the narrow valley below them and the snow-covered ridges angling away, glinting in the clear air, seemed almost mystical. She'd done what she never would have done if she'd believed the newspapers. But she'd called her friend in St. Louis on Miles's credit card, and he'd supplied his driver's license and address and car registration. And there was something comforting, too, in his red hair and wild manner: he was recognizable. He could never do anything in secret.

Miles drove too fast on the curves, but he seemed in control, even when the Jeep slid to the outside.

"Nervous?" he asked. "I'll slow down."

"A little, but I assume you know the road."

"I've driven it a hundred times, and each time is the first." He slowed down as if to soothe her, and pointed through the windshield. "I live over there on that hill," he said. "See the gondola? Now isn't that better than any hotel?"

She had to admit it was. It was a palatial house, modern, wood with golden glass and a soaring roof. Beyond it, the dim moonlight caught the mountains, illuminating dark patches of timber and the steep side canyons. The ski slopes were neat white fingers.

Miles turned right off the main highway, climbed a side road past condominiums and other huge houses. He stopped a mile up, shifted to four-wheel, and revved up a steep snowy driveway. The house materialized at the top of the hill, larger even than it had seemed from a distance — a gaudy lighted bird hovering above the snow.

They leveled off and stopped beside a beaten-up red Volkswagen. "Ah," Miles said, "I'm glad Sheffield is here."

"Who is Sheffield?" Andrea suffered a stab of panic.

"No one to be afraid of," Miles said. He turned off the engine and smiled in the green dashlight. "Sheffield himself is not certain who he is. For a while he did odd jobs just to stay in town for the skiing. He's educated, brilliant in his own way." Miles snapped open the door, but sat for a moment. "I know one thing about him, though. He's never alone."

"He lives here?"

"Sometimes."

Miles got out and collected Andrea's big duffel and skis, while she gazed at the house. She was suddenly elated she'd accepted his offer. At least she still had courage. Her paralegal job was tedious, and she'd lived the past year in the back-and-forth-to-work syndrome. She wasn't afraid. At the same time, she was aware of all she didn't know.

She climbed the wooden stairs to the deck entrance where

Miles had put her skis. He was waiting for her at the door. "Ready?" he asked.

Andrea nodded.

He smiled easily. "Now, when you meet Sheffield, just play along."

Sheffield's skin was pewter in the firelight. With his arm jutting over the corner of the mantel, he gave the impression of a sophisticated man, slightly bored. He waved a greeting at Miles, and at this signal a woman lifted her head over the back of the sofa facing the fireplace. Right away Andrea felt embarrassed for intruding.

The woman had a model's thin face and arms, and rich dark brown eyes. "From Tulsa," Sheffield said, "this is Enid Lambert."

Andrea waited in the doorway while Miles went forward and shook hands politely. "Would anyone like a drink?" he asked. "Andrea?" He turned and looked at her.

"Please."

"Bourbon all right?" He poured two drinks and handed one to her. "This is Andrea Sykes," he said. "Originally from St. Louis, now from New York. We just met in the Denver airport." He smiled as if to assure her nothing would turn out badly.

"Miles was kind enough to offer..."

"A respite," Miles said. "Andrea's one of America's bright young actresses."

Sheffield and Enid Lambert both looked at her, and Andrea felt her face simmer. She was caught between making Miles look foolish and making herself look foolish. She chose to keep silent and do neither.

"So," Enid said, "someone famous."

Miles's red beard twitched. "She's not famous yet," Miles said. "She's not the ordinary person who gets a quick break."

"What have you been in?" Sheffield asked. "Movies or plays?"

Andrea looked at Miles, who now looked quite serious. "You promised you wouldn't tell anyone," she said.

"Sheffield isn't anyone."

She glanced at Sheffield, then at Enid. "Plays," she said.

"One movie, but it was a small role."

"What did you do in the movie?" Enid asked.

"I laughed." Andrea said, and she laughed nervously.

"For the whole time?"

"Once, in this one scene. It wasn't laughing, really. It's more like envy."

Miles crossed the room and went around the sofa. "Let me tell you about envy," he said cheerfully.

"You?" Sheffield said. "You don't envy anyone."

Miles shook his head. "You're wrong about that. As usual, you're wrong."

Andrea barely listened to the men's banter. She was desperately thinking what plays she had heard of or seen, how to fill in the blanks of the lie. Where in New York did she live? Did she know any real actors or actresses? What were the names of the theaters?

"Whom do you envy?" Enid asked Miles.

Miles looked at Andrea. "Her."

"But you've barely met her," Sheffield said.

"Yes, that's exactly it. Andrea can do anything she likes here. She's anonymous. And better yet, she's an actress. She can do any crazy thing without consequences. People will excuse her. Now if I started something — if I ranted in a bar or shouted on the sidewalk about Jesus or went around with loose women — people would say I'd gone berserk. They know me. But if she does that, it's normal. What do people expect of an actress?"

"I don't believe people would call you berserk," Enid said.

"Oh, yes," Miles said. "But not her." He pointed at Andrea. "She's completely free."

The next morning, Andrea got up to a deserted house. She'd spent a restless night. Once she'd awakened with the bizarre idea of running naked through the streets in the middle of a snowstorm. Another time she imagined getting drunk and sleeping with two men at once. She even thought about shoplifting a pair of gloves. Who would know her if she were caught? Who would care in Telluride?

Then her excitement turned to a cold sweat. She wasn't the

kind of person who'd do such things. She'd been dreaming. And besides, what if she were uncovered as a fraud? People like Sheffield and Enid would sneer at her.

But so what? She didn't know them.

Out the kitchen window, the sun fell across the valley onto a ridge of snow. She fixed herself eggs and toast. It was early still. The gondola hadn't started yet. A single blue car was suspended in her vision above the hill.

Perhaps she ought to check into a condo after all. Miles must have some plan in mind for her, and she'd get into trouble. But she was not in trouble yet, and not miserable either. The night before, once the first blush of the lie had passed, she'd felt intoxicated with it. Sheffield had been witty, sarcastic, even tender toward her, and Enid was one of the most beautiful women she'd ever seen. Miles was the complete gentleman. She'd even wished he might flirt with her, but he hadn't, not once. He'd praised her instead, and the whole evening was infused with brilliance.

She made her breakfast of bacon and eggs and Peet's coffee, and Miles came into the kitchen as she was cleaning up her dishes.

He poured himself a cup of coffee. "Good morning," he said. "How did you sleep?'

"Intermittently," she said. "Why did you say all that last night?"

"All what?"

"About my being an actress."

"Sometimes people don't believe you even when you tell the truth," he said.

"But you didn't say the truth."

"You're Andrea Sykes, aren't you?" he asked.

"Yes."

"A name has no weight. An occupation — that's something else."

"You don't even know what I do."

Miles smiled. "You're an actress. Whatever it was you did before has been changed from a millstone to a helium-filled balloon."

He wished her good skiing and went down the hall.

She had a cup of coffee, too, and stood at the window. The

line of the horizon sliced upward through the blue sky, treeless and snow-covered, and when the line seemed most powerful, it stopped abruptly, and blowing snow feathered into the blue.

She skied to the gondola station, took the lift to Mountain Village, and bought a week's ticket at the Tel-ski office. Then she rode the lift to the top of the mountain. The day was brilliant sun and blue sky, the snow dry and the trails perfectly manicured. She skied See Forever. Andrea was not the most elegant skier, but her body possessed a renewed energy important to her. She felt terrific. Her turns were tight, and she skied faster than she remembered from past years at Stowe or Taos. When she stopped and looked out over the expanse of snowy mountains, the heat swarmed in her face, and she found herself laughing at nothing.

Several men noticed her when she rode the gondola up again. One of them was a rancher from Waco, Texas, about forty, nicely dressed. She liked his voice, and when he asked her to ski with him down Misty Maiden, she accepted. At the bottom of the hill, he asked her out for the evening. "I'd be most honored," he said.

"Are you married?" she asked.

"We'd just be having ourselves a good time," he said.

"I take that as a yes," she said. "And my answer is no."

She met another man in the lift line — a younger man in jeans from Salt Lake City. "What do you do?" he asked.

"Paralegal."

"Is that sort of like half a lawyer?"

"It's not..."

"Have you heard the one about the two lawyers in the john?"

"Fuck off," Andrea said.

She skied alone the rest of the afternoon and came down the Telluride Trail at the end of the day with the zoo crowd.

"Meet anyone?" Miles asked. He was standing on the deck, holding something in his hand, and watching her walk up the path from the gondola station.

"No one magnificent."

"How was the skiing?"

"Good, but tiring."

Miles waited for her at the top of the steps, and for a moment, standing above her in that pose and with his eyes in shadow, he looked menacing, as if he were laughing at her. The object in his hand was a club. She mounted the steps slowly, but when she reached the deck, he was relaxed again, and gentle. "I have a date for you," he said, "if you want to go out."

He unrolled the magazine he was holding, turned the page open, and showed her. There was a color photograph of a blond, sunburned man holding skis. A snowy mountain rose behind him. The caption said he was Wyatt Clarkson, Ph.D. in English from Yale who'd come to Telluride to hone his skills in the biathlon.

Andrea looked at Miles, who was facing the ridge fading into shadow across the valley. "I told him you were an actress from New York," Miles said. "You can go or not go. Or you can tell him whatever you like."

Andrea glanced at the photograph again. The prospect of going to the lodge or a bar and getting mugged by strangers paled in her mind. And yet, when she went home, she'd need some stories to tell. What did you do at night?

Miles's expression told her nothing. He was merely offering.

In St. Louis she'd have known how to proceed. She had friends whose tastes she knew. They fixed her up. Or she met men in her work circle, though all of them were paralegals or lawyers or judges. But what were her resources here? She knew only Miles.

"How open did you leave it?" she asked.

"Actually, it was Sheffield's idea," Miles said. "If you're interested, you're to meet him at the Floradora."

On the way to the Floradora, she window-shopped and watched the people. Some of the people watched her, too, and she felt clumsy, as if they were judging her. She hadn't been able to afford new ski clothes — the hotel was so expensive — and St. Louis was not particularly a ski-clothes town. With the money she saved staying at Miles's, why shouldn't she buy something to wear? Maybe nothing too expensive or too daring, but something classy?

She went into Paragon Sports, and a clerk came over. "You have perfect eyes," the man said. "What can I do for you?"

A half hour later, she felt better. She'd bought pale blue stretch pants and a new dark blue sweater. The town seemed more festive. Jeeps and four-wheels moved along the snowy streets. The sidewalk was more crowded. Everyone wanted to do everything quickly, as if the carnival might pull up stakes and leave town.

The Floradora, a saloon resurrected from the mining days, was in the center of town. It was a little dark, but the crowd made up for the dim light. She found Sheffield at the bar.

"Been skiing?"

"Yes. You?"

Sheffield shook his head. "I live here," he said. "Would you like to sit at a table?"

They had the luck of openings and got a table by the window. Andrea felt self-conscious in her new clothes and crossed her arms in front of herself.

Sheffield ordered two bourbons before they sat down.

"How did you know I wanted a bourbon?" Andrea asked.

"If you didn't, I assume you'd have said. Or will you make a scene?"

"I usually don't drink much," Andrea said.

In the decompression of the night before, Andrea hadn't thought much about Sheffield. He had seemed funny, smart, good-looking enough to attract a woman like Enid. But she remembered now what Miles had said. How was it he didn't know himself? He sat before her with a supercilious grin and blue eyes that were tired. He was not someone to fear.

"Where's Enid?" Andrea asked.

Sheffield shrugged. "I just met her yesterday."

"And you didn't like her?"

"She was all right in bed."

The waitress brought their drinks.

"Is that what you do here?" Andrea asked. "Test women in bed?"

"I don't have a job, if that's what you mean."

"You have money?"

Sheffield smiled. "I have Miles."

"He's the great philanthropist," Andrea said.

"What he seems to be, he's not."

Andrea sipped her bourbon. "What does that mean?"

"He's a magician," Sheffield said. "You'd think with his magic he could work out a little happiness for himself."

"Why is he unhappy?"

Sheffield seemed not to hear. He sighed wistfully and looked across the room as if looking for a friend in the crowd. Then he turned to her, and said softly, "What do you really do?"

Andrea felt herself blush first in anger, then in embarrassed relief. She checked the neighboring tables to see whether anyone else was watching her. "Was it that obvious?"

"Enid believed you," Sheffield said. "You did fine. It's just that I know Miles."

"He told me to play along. I didn't know what to expect."

"You have a natural talent," Sheffield said. "If you want to be an actress, be an actress."

Andrea stirred her drink. "I do and I don't. I'm really a para-legal in a law firm. A para-person."

"What does it matter what you really do?" Sheffield asked. "None of the adjectives we apply to anything are true. Is a doctor really hard-working and caring and conservative? Bullshit. I assume from last night you like to drink bourbon. All the details make us create lies, so what difference does it make if you tell me you're an actress?"

"It makes a difference to me," Andrea said.

Sheffield drained his glass and called for another bourbon. "So you like the lie of telling the truth? You okay with your drink?"

Andrea nodded and sipped her bourbon. "What do you know about Wyatt Clarkson?" she asked. "Miles said he was your idea."

"My idea knowing Miles." Sheffield smiled wearily. "Wyatt's likeable. If you want, I'll introduce you."

"I'd like that," Andrea said. "But will he believe me if I tell him a lie?"

Sheffield shrugged. "If you believe it yourself," he said.

❖ ❖ ❖

Sheffield and Mae Jane Lovett from Charleston were sitting with Wyatt and Andrea in the Fly Me To The Moon Saloon. Wyatt Clarkson was like no man she'd ever met. He was not so perfect as his photograph — his hair was not so neatly combed, nor his complexion so smooth, but reality was better than perfection. His face had movement, a twitch of the eye, a raised corner of the sleek mouth, a smile in the dark eyes. He had traveled all over the United States and Europe, had raced in Squaw Valley, Stowe, Zermatt. After graduate school at Yale, he had worked in San Francisco as a house painter to grubstake his first year on the biathlon tour. "I know it sounds odd," he said, "but at that time in my life I would have done anything to train."

"It doesn't sound odd," Andrea said. "Doing what you love is important. I find myself immersed and enchanted in certain roles."

"Sheffield says you've been in the movies."

"Three movies, but only small parts. Jack Nicholson was in one of them."

Andrea looked at Sheffield for his approval. He winked surreptitiously.

"Did you sleep with him?" Mae Jane asked.

Andrea smiled an innocent smile. "I'm not telling," she said. "Let's go to another place."

They skipped from bar to bar. Drinks appeared before she ordered them, and she scolded Sheffield. But she didn't feel a thing. The more she talked, the calmer she was. She told anecdotes she made up about summer stock or about the depressing days when she was out of work. Wyatt listened carefully, and the more convinced she was he believed her, the more she liked him. The more she liked him, the wilder the stories became.

Toward midnight they were back in the Fly Me To The Moon Saloon. She was talking to Mae Jane and asked suddenly, "How can you have a name like Mae Jane?"

"It's just my name," Mae Jane said. "In the South we have names like that."

"Two names?" Andrea heard her own voice harden. "Bobbie Jo, Sara Lee." She giggled. "Mae Bea. Mae Bea not." She laughed

46

and looked into the glittering chandeliers.

"You're drunk," Sheffield said.

"It's a mood," she said. "Actresses have moods."

Sheffield and Mae Jane disappeared around one in the morning, and Andrea was left alone with Wyatt. "I'm having such a good time," Andrea said. "I hate for this to end."

"It doesn't have to end, but we can go home."

"Let's have one more drink," Andrea said.

Wyatt was polite enough to agree.

Andrea ordered a double and drank it purposely and quickly. When the bill was paid, she excused herself to be sick in the women's room.

Wyatt could not have been kinder. "It happens to all of us," he said, driving her to Miles's.

"I'm so sorry," she said. "I wanted to..."

"I hope I'll get to see you again," Wyatt said.

"Of course. I'd love that."

The next day her head ached, and she stayed in bed. She couldn't ski, though she could see through her window the sun was strong on the mountain. Toward noon, Miles tapped on her door. "Andrea?"

She feigned sleep. Miles opened the door and came in.

"Wyatt called," he said. "He asked whether you were still alive. I thought I'd check."

"I'm alive," she said.

"You had a good time?"

"Yes." She paused. "I didn't do anything terrible." She sat up slowly.

Miles stood in the doorway with a glass of water and an Alka-Seltzer. "Apparently Wyatt enjoyed himself."

"Is that what he said?"

"And that you drank a lot."

"I can drink if I want," Andrea said.

"Of course you can," he said easily.

An awkward void rose in the room between them and created a crackle of electricity Andrea had not expected. The comfort she'd felt with Miles withered in his indifference. Miles walked to the window and looked out.

"Is Sheffield here?" she asked.

"I don't know. He didn't come home last night."

A moment passed.

"Do you enjoy this?" Andrea asked.

"What is that?"

"Our spectacle," she said.

Miles smiled at her, then dropped his gaze. "Wyatt wants you to call him, when and if you want to."

She called Wyatt later that afternoon from the telephone in the hallway.

"It was my fault," Wyatt said.

"How was anything your fault?" She heard her voice as angry. "I wanted to drink, and I chose to drink more."

"Let's forget about it then."

"Forget it? Why?" She watched her reflection in the hall mirror — the curve of her body invisible under her loose clothes, the hair to her shoulders as she'd worn it since college. "If I want to drink myself sick, I can and will," she said.

"All right."

"Do you understand me?"

"You can drink as much as you like," he said.

"Or do anything else I want."

"Yes."

"You still want to see me?"

"Why wouldn't I?"

Andrea thought of several reasons. "All right then," she said.

That evening it clouded up. Banks of gray drifted over the mountains from the northwest and slid down over Ilium. Toward nightfall, the snow started, softly at first, then in great gauze sheets.

Andrea's mood lightened as soon as she saw Wyatt at the Floradora. They spoke in a superficial badinage she hadn't known she was capable of. She was more skillful at lying, more confident than she'd ever been in her life. She embellished parties she'd been to (one with Princess Di and Donald Trump), people she'd met

(Tina Turner, Gabriel Byrne, Gary Hart). She invented stories that could never have been true about the old Andrea Sykes.

She did not drink much — just a glass of wine. Wyatt was the one who drank — one Heineken after another.

"When do you have to be back in New York?" he asked.

"When my agent calls."

"Days or weeks?"

"I've been reading a script. Joshua DeKalb is getting a cast together for a movie he's shooting in Montana. They know who I am and what I can do."

"What can you do?" Wyatt asked.

The clarity had left his eyes; his mouth loosened around the edges. She hesitated, as though wondering how to tell a secret, and looked around the crowded bar. There were other men as good looking as Wyatt or Sheffield, men whose stories she didn't know. Did they live here? She turned back and smiled. "I'd be a hitchhiker willing to kill."

Wyatt grinned. "Great! I can see it!"

"I may have to leave town soon."

"Not before tonight, though." Wyatt leaned forward.

"No," Andrea said. "Why don't we make dinner at your place?"

Wyatt ordered another Heineken and took it out under his coat.

They trekked arm-in-arm down Main Street through the snow. She loved the gray air, the brilliance of snow cascading through the street lamps, the touch of snow against her face. She put her head on his shoulder. "Will you ski one day with me?" she asked.

Wyatt reeled away from her and drank from his beer. He stopped on the sidewalk and studied a snowy blue Cadillac parked near the corner. Snow settled on his hair, his eyelashes. His expression turned bitter.

"What are you doing?" she asked.

Wyatt stared at the car. He walked around and tried the driver's door. It was locked. He brushed snow from the windshield and looked in. He went around to the grille and drank the rest of his beer.

Then he hurled the empty bottle as hard as he could into the windshield. The glass starred in front of the steering wheel: tiny white lines shot out from the point of impact. Then he turned and ran.

Andrea waited in the entry to Wyatt's condominium for an hour, watching the snow cut through the window lights across the street. She thought of calling Miles to find out if he knew where Wyatt might go, but she didn't want to talk to Miles. She didn't want a simple answer; she didn't want to cruise bars.

So she waited. Time slowed down. She thought how far away her office was, her girlfriends, the small apartment near where her mother lived. The snow kept on hard, covering the streets, the cars, the trees, making the mountain invisible.

Wyatt did not look at her when he passed. He brushed by and unlocked the door, leaving it open for her to follow or not. He didn't seem surprised to see her.

She closed the door quietly behind her. She turned on the light and crossed the room to open the curtains.

"Leave the curtains closed," he said. "Turn off the light."

She turned off the light.

"I should tell you something," he said.

"You don't have to tell me anything," she said. She unbuttoned her blouse.

She moved closer, took her blouse off. It was simple to do such a thing.

"I want to be honest," he said.

She unbuckled his belt, unbuttoned his jeans, kissed him. She was an actress. She knew he was willing, and she had done this many times before.

She woke to a bright sky with a full sun. Wyatt slept curled toward her with a beer-swollen face and his hair sticking up every which way. She smiled at this new image of him.

She got up and went to the bathroom, then came back and stood naked at the window. She wanted him to see her. A foot of snow had fallen outside, and people were shoveling out their cars.

Wyatt stirred in the bed: she knew he was looking. She tried to be casual about her body as she turned around.

Wyatt wasn't smiling as she thought he'd be. His expression wasn't admiring, but puzzled.

"What is that look for?" she asked.

"I've never slept with an actress before."

"Well, don't look at me that way."

"You're looked at all the time," Wyatt said.

"I've acted. I've posed. That's different."

Andrea reached for the sheet, but he pulled it away from her. She looked for her clothes, but they were in the living room. She was naked then, when before she wasn't.

"Do you want to go skiing today?" he asked.

She tried to cover herself.

"Doesn't it look perfect out there?"

"You can see it does."

"I don't ski," he said.

"What do you mean? You said you'd go with me."

"I can't ski. I never said I'd go."

He handed her the sheet, and she drew it around her.

"Miles showed me the article about you in that magazine."

"I stood on some skis," Wyatt said. "Someone took a photograph. The writer made up a phony story."

"You didn't train for the biathlon?"

He shook his head.

"No Ph.D from Yale?"

"My name isn't even Wyatt Clarkson," he said.

He reached for her hand.

"Don't," she said.

"Look, I wanted to tell you..."

She turned away. "Don't. Don't."

She found Miles in a small room under the eaves. He was sitting at an old IBM typewriter, a half-finished page rolled into the carriage. When she came in, he looked startled. His beard quivered, and he swiveled in his chair toward her. "You found out about Wyatt," he said.

"Wyatt told me the truth."

A wisp of a smile creased Miles's face. He paused. "Did you

tell him about you?"

"No."

"Then you're safe."

"Safe?"

"Yes, safe."

For a moment they looked at one another. Then she understood.

"You haven't been unhappy, have you?"

"No."

"Bored?"

"Not for a minute since I've been here."

"Haven't you been amused?"

The word was not right. Amused. She had been more than amused, more than entertained. Challenged. "You've made all this up," she said.

Miles smiled. "I gave you a place to stay," he said. I left you alone."

Andrea was silent.

"Did I force you to do anything?"

"No." She whispered the word.

Miles swiveled back and faced his typewriter.

"But why?" Andrea asked.

Miles typed a few words.

"Sheffield, too?" Andrea said.

Miles lifted his shoulders in a sigh. "No one knows who Sheffield is," he said. "He's a graduate of Princeton. A skier..."

Andrea nodded. "I'm welcome to stay, then?"

Miles typed more words, then turned and smiled. "Of course. As long as you like. Oh, I know you have your job to get back to. But the summers here are cool. It rains in the afternoons. The mountains are beautiful. The meadows in the high country are green, such a brilliant green."   ▲▲▲

The Spirits of Animals

The next day we were going bow hunting for elk in the wilderness up off the Last Dollar Road, and that Friday Wayne Carson and Jorge Martinez, two friends of mine from high school, drove over from Norwood. Wayne had been pretty crazy for a couple of weeks because his wife, Carol, had run off to Junction with a pizza delivery boy. He'd broken up a bar and had bashed in the windshield of a Mercedes, and his probation officer was threatening to send him back to county jail. Jorge thought Wayne could get interested in killing something, so we were going to spend the night in my trailer in Placerville and get up before dawn on Saturday, which was opening day.

That evening we organized our gear — oiled the eccentric wheels of the compounds, tightened and waxed the bowstrings, filed the broadheads to razor sharp. Our camouflage was laid out. Wayne and Jorge had already picked up sandwiches at the Subway. In the morning we'd make a thermos of coffee and be gone.

We were sitting around the trailer and Jorge suggested we go into Telluride. "Make some laughs," he said. "Have a couple of cold ones."

"There are cold ones in the fridge," I said.

"But in there no women." Jorge smiled. "You want to sit around this dump all your life, man?"

He was right, the place wasn't very clean. There were books

and magazines scattered all over, dirty clothes in the corner, dishes on the counter. There was never much reason to straighten up. When I got home from the construction site, I'd drink a couple of beers and doze and read.

"Do us all good, man," Jorge said. "Wayne needs to hear some music. Soothe the savage beast."

We took Wayne's truck. I figured we'd drive up Keystone Hill, throw in a couple of hours at the Eagles Bar, or maybe catch the Braves' play-off game on TBS, and be back by eleven. I knew how Jorge's excursions for women usually went.

It was a cool night with a breeze coming down the river. Jorge kept the window open, and we could smell the smoke from the Yellowstone fire in Wyoming five hundred miles to the north. That's what people said it was, though it was hard to imagine smoke traveling so far. Smoke drifted through the headlights and made the red sandstone grayish.

If it had been deer season, we'd never have gone in. Telluride wasn't exactly a hunter's town — too much money and glitz. But it was August and another Friday night. The festival goers were going to be there for whatever festival it was — jazz, bluegrass, film. You name it, and Telluride had a festival. They should have had a festival for fornication. That's what Jorge thought.

As it turned out, there was no festival, but a dance at the Elks Club. There was a live band at the Fly Me To The Moon Saloon so we went there. We settled into a table in the corner and ordered pitchers.

Then Wayne asked for a round of Slivovitz. That was the first bad sign. When Wayne was on edge, he gave his money away, but there was no pleasure in it. You didn't know how or why, but you owed him, and when he would collect was anybody's guess.

We drank our beers and shots and listened to the music — a band called Super Iguana — and between sets we talked. Jorge was a pipefitter for a natural gas company, married with three children, though that didn't slow him any. And he could tell a good story. He told one about a left-handed woman giving a blowjob that made me laugh. I swear Jorge could make a nun forget about God. But he couldn't reach Wayne.

Around ten, a few women came in from the Elks dance.

They didn't belong in the Moon. They had on dresses and jewelry and had their hair done up. There were maybe eight or ten of them — brightly colored, pretty women all of them. Jorge went over to the bar, and in a few minutes he'd brought two of them over to the booth.

"This here's Wayne," Jorge said to them. "He's a ranch foreman over in Norwood. And this other one's Jimmy who knows about everything there is about construction. Jimmy's smart, too. He was fourth in our class."

"Fourth boy," I said. "And we had a small class."

"Jimmy Buffett," the one in the dark red dress said. "You look like Jimmy Buffett."

"This is Ruth," Jorge said, "and Ruth's friend."

Ruth had short, blondish hair and a lopsided smile that was more hard than friendly. "There wasn't any good music at the Elks," she said. "Not so you could dance. We came here for a weekend getaway with a group from Alamosa."

"Why don't you girls sit down?" Jorge said. "Slide over there, Wayne."

Wayne moved to the corner, but he didn't look too happy about it. Ruth slid in, and then Jorge, and the other woman sat next to me, not too close.

She was prettier than Ruth, I thought — dark hair, nearly black, a round face, brown eyes — and quiet. When I asked her name, she said Cacky. That was all. She looked part Hispanic, which wasn't unusual around Alamosa, but there was something uncommon about her eyes. They were too dark, or maybe angry for a cause — something that made her appeal to me. She had on a tan dress and three bracelets on one wrist.

The bar gained momentum with the arrival of the women. People danced and moved around. Wayne ordered another round of schnapps.

The women had never drunk schnapps before, but they seemed eager to learn. At least Ruth did.

"The best way to drink shots," Jorge said, "is without using your hands." He picked up his glass in his teeth and snapped his head back. Ruth did the same, though she coughed and laughed, and dropped the glass on the table when it was empty.

Jorge, the gentleman, gave her some beer to swallow.

Cacky wouldn't talk much. She sipped her drink and stared at the couples on the dance floor. I could tell Wayne bothered her. He didn't like it when Ruth spilled a little beer, and we had to sop it up with napkins. He glowered from the corner. He ordered more Slivovitz. His head nodded, and just when it seemed he might pass out, he woke again to see what he'd missed.

Cacky, though, made no move to leave or to find anyone else. Neither did she move any closer to me.

"So what do you do?" I asked. "I heard Ruth say you worked in Monte Vista."

"I'm from Arizona," she said. "Ruth and I work for the wildlife service."

I pictured her emptying trash barrels, or working behind a counter at the visitors' center.

"We count cranes," she said.

"Cranes that fly?"

Cacky nodded. "Sandhills and whoopers. We're doing a migration census."

"And where do the cranes come from?"

"Idaho, Montana, Alberta. It's a little early still, but they'll start to move pretty soon."

Jorge and Ruth got up to dance. I looked at my watch.

"You have somewhere to be?" Cacky asked.

"Hunting," I said. I looked at Wayne whose head was on the table. "We have to be out early morning, first light."

"Hunting birds?"

"Elk."

Cacky's eyes brightened. "I know elk," she said.

Jorge and Ruth came back locked arm in arm.

"It's almost eleven," I said. "We should get Wayne home."

"That's Wayne's way of having a good time," Jorge said. "We can't go yet."

"Maybe we can move the party," Ruth said. "Do you all have a place to go?"

Jorge looked at me. "We do, don't we, Jimmy?"

The next thing I knew we were hoisting Wayne into the truck. He was a big man, six two, and already with a gut. We propped him against the window on the suicide. Jorge and Ruth climbed into the bed of the truck where they settled in among the sacks of feed and toolboxes Wayne carried loose. Cacky had no choice but to get into the front seat between Wayne and me. She never once said she didn't want to go.

We started out of town slowly — 15 is the limit — and then got out onto the flats where smoke hung in the air. Cacky might have driven their car, or Ruth's I guess it was — there was a question how they were going to get back to it. But she didn't, and events moved along without regard to tomorrow.

We passed the road to the ski area and Lizard Head Pass and went on down Keystone, curving along the smoky cliffs. I imagined flames leaping up through brush and around geysers and tons of ash pouring into the clear starry sky in Wyoming.

Then we were in the blank darkness of the canyon. Now and then I glanced over at Wayne passed out against the window. But I saw Cacky. She was staring ahead at the road, but not seeing it, the way I sometimes stared at the walls of my trailer, or at a line on a page without reading it. It wasn't the liquor. She had nursed her one schnapps and had drunk only half a beer. I wondered what she meant to have happen, why she'd let Ruth talk her into coming.

The truck shimmied, as if it were bearing through a gust of wind, and I let up on the gas. A tool box clanked in back. Cacky looked around, and in the rearview I saw Jorge bare-assed on his knees. Ruth had her dress up around her waist, one leg over a sack of feed, and her arms around Jorge's back.

Cacky didn't say anything. Jorge and Ruth stopped after a few minutes, and the ride smoothed out again. We went through Sawpit and skittered some gravel under the tires. In the far distance the pole light above my trailer winked out of the smoky sky.

"What do you know about elk?" I asked finally.

I felt her smile, felt her look at me, though I couldn't see her face in the shadow. There was quiet in the car. No one breathed, even Wayne.

"I know they're whirlwinds and spirits," she said softly. "They hide in the mountains, and their horns are made of silver."

2.

It was still dark when we got up the next morning. Jorge and Ruth had taken my bed so Cacky and I ended up in the living room — she on the sofa the last few hours, and I on the floor. I woke Jorge, who was groggy from booze, and let Ruth sleep.

Wayne came in from the truck. Cacky had on Jorge's jeans and my camouflage jacket. "What the fuck is she doing?" Wayne asked.

"Going with us," I said.

"In dancing shoes?"

"She can drive the Jeep back around from Devil's Quarry," I said. "She doesn't need shoes. We won't have to backtrack to the truck."

Wayne didn't like anything he didn't decide first. He got his gear and went out to the truck to wait for Jorge. Jorge took his time. He pulled on his camouflage — two shades of brown and tan, no green — and brushed his face with charcoal. We had a bite to eat. I'm sure the wait out in the cold didn't help Wayne's disposition.

Cacky and I led in the Jeep because I knew the country better than Wayne. We took 64 East uphill along Leopard Creek toward Dallas Divide. We passed a few lights on all night, and then the remains of the hut at Ski Dallas. I slowed and panned the headlights across the green sign for Last Dollar and swung right.

The night before still addled me. I remembered Jorge and Ruth leaning against each other in the yard like two dazed fighters while I unlocked the trailer door. It was chilly, and Cacky shivered beside me on the porch. Then we were inside. The living room was as we'd left it, with our gear all over. I moved a bow and a quiver from the sofa so people could sit down, but Jorge took Ruth down the hall to the bedroom.

Cacky stayed by the door. "You hunt with bows?" she asked.

That had been a revelation to her. She wanted to know all about it — how the compound bows worked, how we tracked game, where we went. It wasn't that we took the hunting that seriously, I told her. We shot a deer once in a while, but none of us had ever got an elk. She lifted one of the bows, felt its weight, the tension of the string. She had strong shoulders and drew the compound easily.

"Do you have an extra one?" she asked.

"I have an old recurve," I said.

"Can I go with you?"

I managed a smile. "Dressed like that?"

"I could borrow some clothes."

Cacky put the bow down. I had no particular objection to her going. There was no reason a woman couldn't cover as much territory as a man. But I shook my head. "Wayne would be pissed," I said.

"Do you listen all the time to Wayne?"

I didn't answer. I didn't always listen to Wayne, but I'd known him a long time and most of the time you had to listen to him. I'd known him longer than I'd known Cacky. And I was tired, too tired to argue.

That was when Cacky came over to where I was near the sofa. She unzipped the back of her dress and slid her arms from the sleeves. "Please," she said. "I'll be quiet."

She let the dress fall.

It was eerie driving the Jeep in the dark through terrain I knew well in the daylight. It was a bleak country in some ways — aspen glades down low along the road and then spruce higher up toward the mountains, but open territory, too — swales of grass, vistas toward the west and north, only a few ranch lights in all that space. The Jeep had only one good headlight, and we couldn't see much of the country — sage here and there along the road, a fenceline, an outcropping of rock, aspens glittering green in the headlight. The stars.

Wayne's headlights jumped and shifted in the rearview as the truck tires hit rocks. He stayed back a ways because of the dust, and when the road got steeper he dropped back even farther.

Wayne had always had a streaky temper. I remembered once he hit his wife with a horseshoe because she'd said 'fuck you' to him, and another time in a bar he'd belted someone over whose quarter was up next for eight-ball. It didn't matter to Wayne who was right. The time I remembered best was in the state football play-offs. Wayne had kicked a field goal, and Norwood was up 10-7 in the fourth quarter against Limon. Limon was driving, but we had them fourth and three on our 27-yard-line. They ran a sweep. I came up from linebacker and tackled their halfback for a loss, but Wayne, trailing the play, piled on and broke the ballcarrier's leg. With the penalty, Limon got first down on our 12, and we lost 14-10. That was how Wayne did things.

We traversed the flank of an invisible hill, then crested the plateau on a narrow, pock-marked track wide enough only for a single car. Cacky and I didn't speak. It was as though our fatigue was so pervasive that nothing made sense right then. Two people — total strangers — met in a bar, and then through fluky circumstances ended up making love on the floor of a trailer. Now we were careening over ruts and rocks on our way to hunt elk. It seemed preposterous. Yet to me it had some meaning beyond fatigue, beyond mere coincidence. I wanted it to.

We stopped at the turnoff at a T and got out and waited for Jorge and Wayne. There was no sign for which way to go. It was a place the locals knew, with just a trail leading south into the dark timber. This was where we would leave the truck.

Our plan was to take the Jeep another three miles cross country. We'd drop Wayne off at the head of a wide canyon we called The Scoop, and then Jorge lower down in the meadows. I'd drive the Jeep with Cacky to Devil's Quarry and walk back over two ridges, pushing the elk ahead toward the two of them. It was a strategy that seemed logical, but it had never worked.

"So where are your friends?" Cacky asked. "I thought you were supposed to station yourselves before it got light."

"They'll be coming."

I poured coffee from the thermos and leaned against the front bumper. Light was beginning to seep up over the peaks to the east of us.

Finally Wayne's headlights appeared over a rise and scattered down into the willows along Spring Creek. He bounced hard over rocks on the upslope and pulled up dust when he stopped. When the dust settled, they got out.

"Jorge got sick," Wayne said. "The weak little shit."

"Too much love," Jorge said. He smiled and went behind the

truck and threw up again.

Wayne climbed into the front seat of the Jeep where Cacky had been. "Let's go," he said. "We haven't got all day."

Cacky and Jorge rode in back. We drove south and west along the contour through the gray smoky dawn.

The mood was somber from hangovers and fatigue, or maybe from some unspoken anger. Except for Cacky. She wanted to know more about the bows, what the arrows were made of, why the strings had silencers on them. "Have you scouted this place?" she asked. "How do you know there are elk here?"

"Jimmy comes up here all the time," Jorge said. "He brings his girlfriends here."

"So you know there are elk?" Cacky asked me.

"Lots of elk," I said. "but none with silver horns."

Wayne got out at the headwall of The Scoop. In other years we'd had a ceremonial shot of bourbon for luck, though it had never brought us any. But that morning no one mentioned it. Wayne grabbed his bow and the back quiver he liked with six razorheads in it. Before I'd even thought about the bourbon, he was striding away down the hill. He didn't turn or wave.

"That Wayne," Jorge said. "No wonder his wife left him."

Cacky climbed into the front seat again, and we turned back west, skirting the ravine on what was barely a road, and coming downhill a little through spruce and aspen. The headlight ricocheted through the trees.

Then we were in the top of the meadow, bouncing over grass clumps and stones. I stopped at the edge and let Jorge out. He didn't look so good. He was sweating and shaking.

"Sure you're okay?" I asked.

"You drive them to me, and I'll pick them off," he said.

I held out my hand, and he slid his palm across mine. Then he snugged down his camouflage hat.

Cacky and I went on. By then it was nearly full light, and I snapped off the headlight. We rode listening to the revving engine and the scrape of the bottom of the Jeep over rocks and logs. In about half a mile I pointed to a collection of boulders. "That's Devil's Quarry," I said. "You can drive straight downhill and intersect with the lower road. Think you can find the truck?"

"But I'm going with you," Cacky said. "I want to try the bow."

I looked at her. She had such an eager and determined expression I knew I couldn't order her to do anything. "For a while maybe," I said.

We drove up the nose of the ridge as far as we could, and then I turned the Jeep around and let the engine die. For a minute we listened to the breeze slide over the boulders.

The sun was rising then into thin smoke. It was quiet, cold. I leaned across the seat and kissed Cacky on the lips. She didn't object, but she didn't help, either. She kept her eyes open.

After a moment, she broke away. "I thought we were hunting elk," she said, and she cracked open the door and climbed out.

The breeze uphill was cold, and I buttoned my jacket. I broke off a spruce branch and rubbed the smell into my palms and across my face.

"Cover the human scent," I said.

Cacky did the same.

I strung up my old 45-pound recurve for her — a fiberglass model I'd shot a deer with once over on the Silver Shield by Ouray. A recurve didn't take so much experience as a compound, but it took more strength to pull it. The bow still had a bowsight on it, which was useful, and I'd sighted it in the week before in case my compound broke down.

Cacky had a good instinct with a bow. I gave her three broadheads with damaged feathers to shoot at an anthill, and she barely missed with the first two and drove the third center left.

"How're your feet?" I asked.

"Cold."

"You'll warm up when we walk. We'll head up this ridge, then traverse the ravine and come down through those trees." I pointed across the ravine to a stand of spruce. "Elk like the dark timber."

We walked up the ridge — mostly talus and downed, rotted timber — and generally made our way toward the head of the ravine where it was not so steep. Now and then Cacky stopped to get her bearings or to look at some animal track, and once she pointed out a Pine Grosbeak — a robin-sized pink bird — at the top of a young spruce tree.

But mostly we kept moving. We angled into the scree of the ravine and traversed along a game trail back up the other side. Cacky's shoes were a liability: she couldn't walk fast. I hoped they were a way to get her to turn back sooner rather than later to the Jeep.

When we got into the spruce and boulders on the other side of the ravine, I stopped all of a sudden.

"What is it?" she asked.

"I smell elk."

"What should we do?"

"We should keep quiet. The wind's coming uphill."

I moved forward cautiously through the boulders and into the deeper trees. We emerged into a clearing where we could see a little. The elk — five cows and a nice four-point bull — were on a steep pitch of trees about a half mile away moving slowly. They were upwind and hadn't caught the drift of us.

"You head straight at them. Slowly. I'll circle to the right. If I can't get a shot, we can push them toward Jorge and Wayne."

It was a slow dance. Cacky picked her way through the trees. I followed a game path higher up and we circled in mirror image. It was impossible to guess what the elk would do. I'd seen them run when I approached into a headwind and carried no weapon, and I'd seen them run when a car backfired two miles away.

But that morning they stayed put. Maybe the Yellowstone fire had scrambled their senses. Maybe the bull was lazy or sick. We were able to sneak in as close as I'd ever been to an elk. Cacky was off maybe fifty yards to my left.

I took an arrow from my bow quiver and nocked it on the string. Any moment I expected the bull to catch our scent and take off. I moved closer, and at sixty yards I knelt down and took aim. The bull was facing away from me. I didn't like rear shots, so I waited a few seconds for him to turn. The sun glanced from the aluminum arrow. I squinted past my bowhand, closing out everything except a spot on the bull's shoulder.

Then Cacky clapped her hands.

I was as startled as the elk, but they were quicker. They jerked alert and were at full speed by the second or third step. I let the arrow fly, more from instinct than aim, and it sailed wildly over the bull's pale rear end.

I looked over at Cacky who was standing, hands on hips, watching the elk.

"Aren't they beautiful?" she called out. "It would be a shame to kill the spirit of an animal."

3.

There was no sense crying. The elk were gone. I started down the slope, angling toward the meadow where Jorge was. It was a good mile. I walked fast, hoping to keep the elk ahead of us, not worrying about where Cacky was. It had been my first good chance in four years to shoot an elk. Wayne, Jorge, and I had spent days waiting and stalking, sweating and freezing, camouflaged and scented up with musk or dung. Elk were hard to hunt because they liked steep terrain and were skittish and strong. When they got anxious, they vamoosed. There I was with a fair chance, a real chance, and Cacky had purposely spooked them.

I looked back once to see where she was, but she wasn't headed back to the Jeep where she should have been going. She was in the trees, but climbing higher toward the top of the ravine. She stopped as if she were having trouble with her shoes. Or maybe she'd cut herself on a stone. She was bent over and rubbed her ankle.

I didn't care about Cacky. I should never have got mixed up with her; I should never have brought her along. A quarter mile farther on I reached the edge of the meadow and scanned for Jorge. He was asleep on a little hill in the shade, just at the top of the clearing. Through the muddled glass he looked peaceful, more peaceful than I ever was, a man without worry. He had a wife and family and a Catholic God to forgive his sins. He obviously hadn't seen the elk.

I yelled to him, and he stood up on the hill and waved. I motioned for him to meet me on the other side of the meadow.

I liked the meadow. It was a broad expanse of high grass with tracks all over — signs of what animals had passed there — deer and elk, and in a little wash, a larger track, a bear maybe. In the middle of the meadow I found the dry carcass of a fawn. Animals died too of starvation, disease, deformity. They had no doctors to go to.

The sun was up then, and it was warm. Sweat rolled under my camouflage jacket. Jorge joined me near a stunted pine tree on the far side of the meadow.

"There were six of them," I said. "We pushed them to you."

"I was ready," Jorge said. "But they were pretty far away."

"I saw how ready you were."

Jorge smiled. "You scared them yelling at me."

He had recovered a little and nudged me with a pint of Yukon Jack. I took a swallow and felt the burn.

"Where's Cacky?" he asked.

"I don't know where she went," I said. I took another hit of the Yukon Jack, and looked up toward the cliffs. The air was oddly translucent, like looking through quartz.

"How was she?" Jorge asked.

"Who?"

"Who do you think?"

I knew what he meant. "It didn't happen," I said. "We went to sleep."

Jorge took the bottle and drank and wiped his mouth on his sleeve. "She's Indian," he said. "That's what Ruth told me."

"What kind of Indian?"

Jorge stared at me. "Shit, man, I don't know. What difference does it make?"

It seemed it ought to make a difference, or no difference, depending how you looked at it. Everything ought to make a difference or not. It must have made a difference to Cacky, which explained some things.

Jorge capped the bottle and put it back into his pocket. "Let's get an elk and go home," he said. "Ruth's waiting."

The soft ground in the trees west of the meadow yielded no tracks. It was anybody's guess where the elk had gone, so Jorge and I split up. He took the lower route, out and around, and I went higher along the ridge. I climbed to a ledge and worked my way into the spruce. I couldn't see Cacky. She must have been above me in the trees or over in the next ravine between me and Wayne.

I wondered about her: why had she wanted to hunt, or as it was, not to hunt? How had she grown up? In Arizona there were Navajos, Hopis, Pimas, Papagos, and several groups of Apaches. My guess was she was Apache, a warrior.

From up higher smoke ribboned the sky above the whole Uncompahgre Plateau to the north. I was used to the clear view — high clouds, rolling hills, the distant peaks — but that morning the only landmark visible was a rock formation I called The Arch. It wasn't an arch, really — no open space underneath, but the shape of it was right. It was a little above The Scoop and was silhouetted in the whitish sky.

I stood for a long time watching. That's what I did in my life.

Then Cacky called.

My first thought was she had wounded an elk, but that was absurd. If she wouldn't let me shoot one, she wouldn't shoot one herself. Or would she? I came off the tree-line full tilt.

I ran awkwardly, keeping the bow and arrows tucked in my bow quiver tight to my body. I two-stepped into a shallow ravine and up a grassy slope. I felt my legs soften on the uphill.

At the edge of The Scoop I clambered up to a rocky outcropping where I could see out and across. My whole body was shaking, and my breath was gone. Cacky was on the hillside on the far slope, and she had the recurve drawn on Wayne.

Wayne was on the same contour, twenty feet from her, one leg lower down the slope than the other. He had stripped off his camouflage and was shirtless, still holding his bow at his side. At his feet, with an arrow in its shoulder, was a dead coyote.

Wayne saw me and lifted his head, but he didn't make any sudden move. "Tell her to ease off," he said. "Do something."

I didn't know what I could do. I glanced around for Jorge, but he hadn't appeared yet at the bottom of the ravine. It would have taken Cacky only an instant to release the bowstring, and Wayne would be hurt bad or dead. She was close enough not to miss.

I climbed down through the rocks and onto the hill and approached Cacky from the side, so she could see me clearly without having to give up her position. I dropped down a little lower and edged along toward the dry streambed in the center of The Scoop. When I reached the bottom, I angled up to a point between her and Wayne, but lower.

Then I sat down. The ground under me was warm from the sun. I laid my bow on the dry clay.

"What the hell," Wayne said. "What are you doing, Jimmy?"

I didn't answer. Wayne knew his predicament. Such a situation was created by agreement, it seemed to me: Wayne admitted the power of the weapon, and Cacky was determined to use it. Calling a bluff was tough. The only variable was how long Cacky could hold the tension of the recurve.

The coyote was a thin one. Its head was away from me, but the shoulder, the broadest part, was barely as wide as the rump. There were marks on the ground higher up where the coyote had fallen, and Wayne's footprints coming down the slope toward it.

I measured Cacky. Her face was hard-set, pretty, too, her lips taut. One eye was narrowed against the bowstring. She didn't look at me. It struck me then what she was doing.

"Why'd you kill it, Wayne?" I asked.

"What the hell is wrong with you?" Wayne said. He turned his head just enough to look at me.

"I want you to tell me."

"You know fucking why."

I smiled, though it wasn't a smile.

Wayne stared at me. "You're going to let her keep me here?"

"I don't see that I'm letting her do anything."

"Some kind of payment, is that it?" Wayne asked.

I thought about payment. In a way it was a payment, though not in the way Wayne meant. And it was more than that. "Are you going to tell me or not?" It was something I needed to know, too.

Wayne shifted his weight carefully from one foot to the other. He looked at Cacky. Her bow hand was trembling from holding the string.

"She isn't going to shoot me," Wayne said.

Then I picked up my bow, stood up slowly, and fitted an arrow to the string. I drew and took aim at a spot of the coyote's blood on Wayne's chest. "She isn't going to shoot you," I said, "but I might."

Cacky lowered the recurve and let off on the string.

Wayne looked at me.

"Drop your bow, Wayne," I said.

Wayne held his stance for a few seconds, then let the bow slide from his hand along the string until the concentric wheels at the end caught his fingertips. The bow spun across the clay and skidded to the bottom of the ravine.

"Now back up the hill."

He took a step backward. I raised my bow, following the spot of blood.

Wayne backed up another step.

I meant to say something more then, to Cacky more than to Wayne, something about the spirits of animals or love, but she wouldn't have understood. So I didn't say anything.

Wayne backed up the hill. When he was out of good range, when maybe he could have dodged my arrow, he turned and scrambled up into the trees.

4.

That afternoon I took Cacky and Ruth and Jorge back up to Telluride. Clouds had risen in the northwest and drove hard over the mountains. Rain slanted in gray curtains in front of the oncoming headlights of cars. I imagined water collecting in the gullies and ravines, washing over the meadow, erasing tracks.

We rode in intermittent conversation, mostly Jorge trying to make me sound good to Cacky. He felt sorry for me. "He builds fireplaces like Michelangelo," he said. "And foundations — shit, can Jimmy pour concrete."

"I'm hoping not to go on welfare this winter," I said.

"The man has ideas," Jorge said. "He reads."

The storm shifted east, and where we were in the valley, the clouds broke apart. As we topped out on Keystone Hill, a cool new light flowed down over the sandstone and the pastures. The air was washed of smoke. We drove into town, though the highway was still slick from rain.

I left Jorge off at Rose's Market just into town where he was going to call his wife in Norwood to come and get him. He kissed

Ruth goodbye. Then I drove into town.

I turned on Pine and worked my way through a neighborhood of refurbished houses. Some of the sprinklers were still going on the lawns and flower gardens.

"What's wrong with you two?" Ruth said. "Can't you be polite and talk?"

"We're polite," Cacky said. "We're just tired."

"You aren't going to tell me what happened up there?"

"I already told you," Cacky said. "We didn't shoot an elk."

They had left their car down by the post office by St. Paul's, and I double-parked. Ruth got out and let Cacky and me be alone. I let the engine run.

There wasn't much to say. I suppose I thought making love ought to be love, at least a little, but I didn't know what Cacky thought. I told her I wanted to see her again, and she nodded, meaning neither yes nor no.

"You should come down to the refuge and watch the cranes," she said.

I promised I would.

Then she kissed me quickly and got out. She passed in front of the Jeep's lone headlight still on from the rain, crossed the street, and got into Ruth's Ford. She waved to me, and then she and Ruth were gone from the parking space and were behind me up the street. I turned off the Jeep and sat a minute in the middle of the street, looking at the gray sunlit facade of the church. I wondered what existed and what didn't, and what I was going to do in the long winter ahead. ▲▲▲

On
the Way
to
California

It's been a week. Priester's been gone a week, and the baby cries for him. Melissa doesn't know she's crying for him, but when the time comes in the evening for Priester to feed her, he isn't there. In the night when she wakes, she thinks it will be Priester who's coming to comfort her. Instead she hears my voice, feels the lighter weight of my hand on her back. She wishes it were his hand, his voice. He calms her. He cajoles her. He sings to her ponderous songs like "The Volga Boatman" and "It's Dark as a Dungeon Way Down in the Mine." Listening at the door, I was always astonished his off-key renditions soothed her. What does she understand of these words, "Yo ho, heave ho" and "Tote that barge, lift that bale?" But she sleeps.

We all drank too much that night. It wasn't the first time: something about Iwamasa inspires us to ignore health and safety. Perhaps it's the battles he and Gwen wage in public; or maybe it's the absurd paintings he does which litter their studio — trout and atomic bombs exploding and prisms of color. What made that night so different from the others? We had dinner downstairs at their place and left our door open upstairs to listen for Melissa if she cried. We drank wine, celebrating the sale of Iwamasa's very-well-used Dodge. (The week before it was finding my earring.) What I remember was Priester at the open window watching the wind shake the cottonwoods across the street.

"It's going to be severe," he said. "That's what they said on the radio. It's backed up over the mountains."

The window had no curtain or shade so as to let in every ounce of daytime light for Iwamasa's painting. But at night the windows made it a huge space, big as night itself.

"We could turn on the TV," Gwen said.

"No, let's see it live." Priester turned and smiled just as the first lightning cracked over the houses in the distance. He was medium height, thin as a pole so he looked tall, blond hair. He wore black jeans and a T-shirt that said "Rim Rock 37K" on it. He was a sometime runner in the hills west of Durango.

Those same foothills had disappeared early into the clouds and darkness, and an eerie glow of neon glimmered from downtown into the low overcast. The air moving through the open window cooled the room. Thunder banked against the duplex we shared, and two lamps flickered off and then on again. I wondered whether Melissa would waken.

Iwamasa got up and rummaged through a drawer for some candles. "Gwen used to like to make love by candlelight," he said. "She said it made me look bronzed."

"It made him look like Frankenstein," she said. "That's why we stopped."

"We stopped because she liked the candles more than she liked me."

Iwamasa liked to be called The Yellow Man or General Hirohito. He was tall for a Japanese, five feet ten, and sturdy. He wore his straight black hair shoulder length, longer than Gwen's blond curls. He was dressed that night in maroon trousers from a band uniform, a khaki army shirt, and a gray Civil War jacket with epaulets — all culled from military surplus and thrift stores. He wore a saber at his belt.

"Little Hiro," Iwamasa said. "That's what we're going to name our child. The American Hiro. We'll wrap him in the flag of the Rising Sun."

"What if it's a girl?" I asked.

"Who would have a child with you?" Gwen asked. "That'd be like signing my own goddamn commitment papers. Shit, look at this place. Where would we put a crib? And you don't even have a job."

"I have work," Iwamasa said. "That's better than a job."

"Work?"

"You don't think this is work?" Iwamasa gestured around the room. "You think I do this for my health?"

"This is bullshit," Gwen said. "This stuff is perverse. What do you think, Ellie? Is this art-as-excuse or what?"

"I'm not getting into it," I said.

Iwamasa leaped up and went to his easel by the window.

Priester paid no attention to this. He stared out the window at the night. This was no different from usual. The Yellow Man might rave and prowl and howl at the moon and spill paint out on canvas like blood on the street, but Priester remained serene. He was secretive and wistful. Or maybe it was the talk of children that unnerved him. He loved Melissa, of course, but there was something about having her that troubled him. He'd not been consulted, he said. (Not true.) He hadn't been sure he could adjust. (How can anyone be certain about what hadn't happened yet?) What if something went wrong? (Melissa is a healthy baby.)

Iwamasa stood at the easel for a moment and then turned to Priester. "What do you think?" he asked.

"It's a good night for photographs," Priester said.

"What?"

"Time lapse. Slow everything way down."

"You would take photographs, when there's this?" He grabbed his painting from the easel and held it up.

It was a rainbow trout surfacing in a pool which reflected a mushroom cloud. I thought it full of passion, drama, color, but there was something not right about it, too.

"I sold my camera," Priester said. "You're safe."

"I don't want to be safe," Iwamasa said.

"Like, look at the bomb," Gwen said. "Is that heavy symbolism? Is that DHM or what?"

"What is that?" Iwamasa asked.

"Deep Hidden Meaning."

"That's the message," Iwamasa said. "The consequence for mankind..."

"But not original," Gwen said. "Not new."

A gust of wind whined under the shutters and in the loose wires of the duplex. The window panes clattered and shrank back to silence. Then a bolt of lightning struck close by, and thunder reverberated through the room.

Melissa cried.

Priester volunteered to go upstairs, and when he left the room, Iwamasa closed the window. The studio was quieter. Gwen and Iwamasa struck a truce for the moment. They kissed.

We heard Priester upstairs speaking in his soft voice to Melissa. "Would you like a story?" he asked. "A song?" as if Melissa could understand words.

But she wasn't crying anymore.

Then he sang:

I'll tell you of a hunter whose life was undone
By the cruel hand of evil at the setting of the sun
His arrow was loosed and it flew through the dark
And his true love was slain when the shaft found its mark.

She had her apron wrapped about her,
and he took her for a swan.
But oh no, and alas —
it was she, Polly Von.

"Why does he sing like that?" Gwen asked. "What happened to 'When You Wish Upon a Star?'"

"God if I know," I said.

"You can see why he does it," Iwamasa said.

"Why?" Gwen asked.

We all listened to the next verse in which the hunter tells the father he's killed the daughter.

Iwamasa looked at me. "You know what I mean."

Gwen drank the rest of her wine. "Don't be fucking inscrutable," she said. "Tell Ellie what you mean."

"I don't..."

"Jesus," Gwen said to me. "I keep thinking, Lord, let Hiro change. He's young still. But Priester is old, isn't he? How old is Priester?"

"Forty almost."

"Forty," Iwamasa said. "that's past the mid-life crisis, huh? He's in afterlife."

"Fill my glass," Gwen said.

"Mine, too," I said.

"Forty's mid-mid-life," Gwen said. "And stop saying stupid things."

"Me?" Iwamasa said. "I'm not the one who's going to California."

"Who's going to California?" I asked.

"No one," Iwamasa said. "It's an allusion."

"Allusion, my ass," Gwen said. "He means Priester said something to him about going to California."

"What did Priester say?" I asked.

"Nothing."

Upstairs Priester started in on a distorted version of "Summertime." He was well off-key, but I imagined Melissa's eyes blinking closed.

Iwamasa opened another bottle of wine — a magnum of table red — and poured the glasses full. We toasted good riddance to The Yellow Man's orange Dodge Hornet into which in the last year he had poured $600, and from the sale of which he netted $65. We deserved the wine and drank more.

In a while, Priester came back downstairs. He paused in the doorway as if he noticed something new about the room. His bristly blond hair stuck up all over his head. He seemed wraith-like, arms and legs hollow. "Who shut out the storm?" he asked.

"Yellow Man," I said. "He thought it would rain."

"Of course it'll rain," Priester said. But he didn't move. He gazed at me with what I took to be a guilty expression, like a criminal who, after taking up a life in a quiet neighborhood, has been found out. "So what did The Yellow Man say?" he asked.

"I'm innocent," Iwamasa said.

"He said you were going to California," Gwen said. "Is that a lie? He tells lies all the time. It's his way of being kind."

A tremor passed through Priester's face. He looked at me, and I started to cry. I don't know why. I didn't mean to. Maybe it was the wine.

Gwen looked at me with exaggerated sympathy. "Men are shits," she said.

"Priester's left three other women before me," I said.

"Three? I rest my case."

"It's not as though I'm unprepared."

Outside, the thunder rippled farther away but all around us, as if it were a hand shaking the house.

"That was years ago," Iwamasa said. "What happened before has nothing to do with now."

"It has everything to do with now," I said.

"But you've been together how long?" Gwen asked.

"Five years. We have Melissa."

"Five years," Iwamasa said. "An eternity, then."

"Why California?" Gwen asked. "That place is the pits."

Priester didn't say anything. We talked around him, despite his presence. Finally he went into the kitchen and came back with a bottle of tequila and sat down in the white, halo-backed wicker chair that Iwamasa, in lighter moments, used as a throne.

"I used to live in Gardenia," Iwamasa said. "It was the poker capital of the world."

"We don't care about you," Gwen said. "We want to know about Priester's other women."

"I'm interested in other women, too," Iwamasa said.

He got up and poured more wine all around, the last of it. Lightning shot down right outside the window and thunder exploded on top of us.

"It's going to be bad," Priester said. "I'm telling you."

He got up and opened the window again, still holding the bottle of tequila. There was no wind or rain. The neighborhood was quiet, dark, even though the street lights were still on. But tension drifted in the night air.

I looked at Priester and then at Gwen, addressing her, but knowing Priester would hear. "It's not that I want a promise of anything," I said. "Who can promise to love another person forever? But I'd like to know why he doesn't speak to me. Why doesn't he tell me?"

"What's to tell?" Iwamasa asked.

"Oh, you shut up," Gwen said.

Iwamasa got up and found a bottle of merlot he'd hidden in the broom closet. "Let's try this," he said. He picked up the corkscrew from the coffee table.

"Where did that come from?" Gwen asked.

"California."

"I mean, how long have you been hiding things?"

"So he wants to go to California," Iwamasa said. "So what?" He levered out the cork from the merlot and looked over at Priester. "Driving or flying?"

"Driving," Priester said.

"You admit it?" Gwen said. "You bastard."

"I'll admit what's true," Priester said.

"If you flew, you could be back here in a couple of days," Iwamasa said.

The rain started. We heard it on the side of the house and in the leaves of the Dutch elm out the window. Little snaps.

"Who were the other women?" Gwen asked me. "Do you know?"

"I know a little," I said.

"He's not serious," Iwamasa said. "Can't you see that?"

"Why isn't he serious?" Gwen asked.

"He has a child," Iwamasa said. "He can't leave."

"Oh God, save us," Gwen said. "No man ever left a child."

"We still have Angie's hairbrush," I said, "and some of her tapes, and her European typewriter with the accent marks on it."

"Goddamn," Gwen said. "Who is Angie?"

"Angie was the one in Kansas City," I said, looking at Priester for confirmation.

Priester drank tequila from the bottle.

"And what happened to Angie?" Gwen asked.

"She got transferred to St. Louis. She worked for Burroughs, and Priester wouldn't go with her. Isn't that right, Priester? You refused?"

"Yes."

"And the one before that?" Gwen asked.

"Let's see. The names don't come to me right away. Priester told me about them years ago. I've never been jealous. They were fictional people to me, like characters in a book. I didn't hold the women against him."

"Maybe you should have," Gwen said.

"There was one in Harrisburg — Kate, I think — and one in Boston."

Iwamasa poured himself the merlot and set the bottle on the table. A car passed in the street, its tires hissing on the wet pavement. A sliver of light knifed down, and then thunder, and then the lights went out.

"Shit," Gwen said.

"Who was it in Boston?" I asked Priester. He was a silhouette at the dark window.

"Helene."

It rained harder, and we listened a moment. The rain splashed on the windowsill, and the black panes above the open window shimmied with the gusts of wind. Priester closed the window, and we heard the smooth rush of water on glass.

Iwamasa lighted two candles which guttered in the air.

"Isn't there a flashlight?" Gwen asked.

"Whoever heard of making love by flashlight?" Iwamasa said.

"We might as well. It only lasts thirty seconds."

Another barrage of lightning slammed down. Melissa shrieked.

Priester leapt from beside the window.

"I'll go," I said.

"I will," Priester said.

"I have to use the bathroom. If I can't quiet her, I'll bring her down."

I took one of the candles, and as I climbed the stairs, held my palm near it to shield it from the draught.

Melissa was hungry. I heated milk on the gas stove and gave her a bottle. That was what she wanted. I had never breast-fed her because I wanted Priester to take part in the feeding, but holding her then, listening to the rain on the roof, I understood it was a trick I'd tried on him. It hadn't worked.

But it was not as though we argued. Not like Iwamasa and Gwen. We got along like most couples, disagreeing now and then, spelling out our boundaries. We quarreled about what to buy at the Safeway, who'd pay for what movie, whether to hike in Mesa Verde or to Highland Mary Lakes near Silverton. None of these quarrels was a reason to leave.

Yet I knew his expression in the doorway. I had read his face at the window. I saw that longing. I heard him sing his songs to Melissa.

After I finished feeding Melissa and putting her back to bed, I lingered by the window in her room, just to be with her, and watched the invisible rain fall into the darkness. On a whim — only it wasn't a whim — I went to the storage closet in Melissa's room and found two portfolios on the shelf. I kissed Melissa and went back downstairs carrying the candle and the two books.

Priester was still at the window where I'd left him. I had hoped Gwen and Iwamasa might have taken their struggles to bed, but they were still there. Gwen looked drawn and weary, but The Yellow Man had taken out his saber and was waving it wildly in the air.

"Put it away," Gwen said. "What are you some kind of samovar?"

"Samurai," Iwamasa said. He clanked the sword on the leg of his metal easel. "You're lucky I don't take this blade to you."

"Unlucky," Gwen said. She turned to me. "How's the baby?"

"Asleep," I said.

I set the candle down by the one already on the table. Iwamasa whipped the sword through the air and lunged at the wall.

"It's been like this since you left," Gwen said.

"These are Priester's," I said. "I thought you'd like to see them." I put the portfolios down beside the candles.

"What are they?" Iwamasa sheathed his sword and came over.

I looked at Priester who didn't move from the window, didn't look around. It was still raining hard, a torrent, and wind raked the trees. Far away a siren squealed. Lightning flashed down again, illuminating Priester's face and the leaves thrashing beyond him in the wind. I knew he'd been drinking tequila.

"They're his portfolios," I said.

That was when he looked around. "You can't show those," he said.

"Why can't I?"

"They're mine."

"They're a history," I said.

Gwen turned the first page before Priester came over.

The woman in the photograph was backlighted so the curve of her naked body was a black line shading toward light. Her hair was short and dark, her lips full, her eyes pockets of shadow.

Gwen turned another page. It was the same woman lying on a wood floor with her back to the camera.

"Don't," Priester said. He stepped to the edge of the table and stopped, trying to keep his tenuous balance. But the tequila was in him, and it was already too late.

Iwamasa held him by the arm. "It's all right," he said. "We're friends here."

"Finally we get to issues," Gwen said. "Who is that?"

"That's Kate," I said. "Kate left us some souvenirs, too. That miniature TV set and some towels."

"Why did you keep them?" Gwen asked.

"You can't just throw stuff away just because it has another woman's fingerprints on it."

"It wouldn't be fingerprints that would bother me," Gwen said.

"Jesus," Iwamasa said. "You left *her?*"

Priester's face was blank, wide-eyed. He was drunk. He wavered a moment, then sank down into the white wicker chair.

Iwamasa squeezed in beside me on the sofa and turned the page.

I was not upset. Pictures were not threats. The page Iwamasa had turned to showed Kate again, sitting naked on the edge of a straight-backed chair, her spine arced like a swan's neck. Iwamasa gave a low whistle.

"Shut up," Gwen said.

"Tell Iwamasa about Kate," I said to Priester.

Priester coughed and blinked. "She was a weaver," he said. "I met her when I bartended at the airport in Harrisburg. After eight months on the job, one day Kate came in... That's all. Ellie makes it sound as though I plotted something."

"Did you?" Gwen asked.

"I planned to leave Harrisburg when I'd saved enough money."

I smiled at Priester, and turned to Gwen and Iwamasa. "That's how he does it. He sits back and waits. He plots. That's how it works — one person has to leave first, right? Priester never takes a risk."

"It's always me," Priester said.

"What happened to Kate?" Iwamasa asked.

Priester shook his head.

The rain had slacked to a drizzle. We were conscious of it. The thunder moved off to the east, toward Vallecito. Then the lights came on suddenly and filled the room.

Iwamasa turned the pages of the book slowly, dwelling on each picture in a way that made Gwen seethe. But they were beautiful pictures. Priester had made them that way.

"So you started in Boston," Iwamasa said.

"Boston, yes," Priester said.

"Who was Helene?" Gwen asked.

I turned several more pages to speed things along. I stopped at a black-and-white of a dark-skinned woman lying on grass and partially covered with blossoms. Her black hair was arranged behind her head, and shadows of tree limbs and tiny leaves crisscrossed her skin.

"Don't tell me," Gwen said.

"She was the first," I said. "Isn't that right, Priester. Helene was the first."

"Yes."

"Tell the story."

"I don't know the story," he said.

"Helene was a street kid," I said. "She jimmied coin boxes in laundromats and arcades."

"She doesn't look like a street kid," Iwamasa said.

"It's hard to tell without clothes," Gwen said.

"That's the point," I said. "Priester makes them look like goddesses."

"Or whores," Gwen said.

Iwamasa reached for the merlot. "How long were you with her?" he asked Priester.

"Year and a half."

Priester got up and stumbled from the chair to the middle of the room.

"And then what?"

"Then nothing."

"That's no answer." Iwamasa got to his feet and drank from the merlot bottle. "That's not the answer we want."

Priester tilted his head as though he were listening to the last of the storm drifting out into the mountains. He slugged more tequila. "East," he said. "The storm is going east."

I closed the portfolio and lifted the second one onto the first. "We have to look at these now," I said. "These are the ones that matter."

I opened the book to a random page somewhere near the middle.

The photograph was of glossy, short-grass hills stretching one after another, defined by distance and gradations of shadow. Clouds rose above the hills. The colors were beige and tan, bleak as the land that made them.

"You can see where water was," I said. "Where the grass is taller, a lighter color."

I paged to another photograph — a single stunted aspen tree with leaves dead or dying on the branches, thirsted or starved, on an empty rocky slope.

More: barns of sunbleached boards falling down, houses on the plains collapsing from the weight of weather, windmills still against the huge sky. I kept turning the pages.

Gwen said nothing. Iwamasa finally edged away from the table and walked to the easel. He drew his saber again.

"You," he said. "You!" He slashed the canvas in the center, then turned and leveled the blade at Priester.

Priester shook his head. Thunder sounded far way, but you had to listen for it.

"California," Priester said. "All my possessions were in the car..."

"Speak up," Gwen said. "Why spare our feelings now?"

"All my possessions..."

"You were going to sneak out," Iwamasa said, raising his sword. "The silent exit."

"Let him talk," Gwen said. "Let him finish."

Priester smiled grimly. "Omissions, you see. Things left out. When I got to California, I was supposed to write."

"Helene?" Iwamasa said.

Priester said nothing for a moment. A drop of water caught light from the street, and silver ran down the windowpane.

"You were supposed to write Helene when you got to California," Iwamasa said. "Is that it? And she was going to meet you."

"That was years ago," Gwen said.

"The car broke down," Priester said. "I ran out of money and had to work. I've taken my time."

"Not to mention being with Kate and Angie and Ellie," Iwamasa said.

"And Melissa," I said.

Priester looked at me. "Helene was never going to come." His words were quiet, slurred with tequila. "I knew that."

I felt time stop for an instant and then start moving again in a new direction. Away from me. I thought of Melissa who would not remember "The Volga Boatman" and "Old Man River." Priester was already gone. He was on his way to California, and I saw the long nights ahead when Melissa would wake in the dark and he would not be there to comfort her. ▲▲▲

A
Way
of
Dying

N o one but a madman forgets who he is, but William Bryce Talbot had lived so long alone in the mountains he no longer thought of himself with a name. "My name meant what my father wanted it to," he said aloud to himself, as if to someone interviewing him. "It might have been a name everyone knew, a famous name..." He stopped. Recently his voice sounded hollow. It broke in the back of his throat like an aspen leaning against another tree in the wind.

He was sitting on the straw mattress in the corner of the one room. The light there had never been good because there was only a single window and the door to let in the sun. He meant to put in more windows and a lock on the door, but one day had led to another, and now he no longer thought of that either, anymore than he thought of his name.

He'd never had a mirror. When he got supplies in town he saw himself in store windows, but always he was shadowy, obscured by the reflections of other things. And people watched him, and he felt uncomfortable watching himself. Sometimes along the stream, he found a still pool, and he knelt and tried to make out who he had become — the dark silhouette with the beard, his wild long hair backlighted by sky and spruce. But his eyes, no matter how calm the pool, were never visible.

"Look at yourself," he said, as if admonishing his reflection.

The water rippled in a murmur of breeze and bled the image. "Stand up," he told himself. "It does no good to see who you are." But standing, looking down at himself from a different, higher angle, he continued to wonder.

He had imagined when he was ready to die, God would hurry up to him like an harassed servant and ask him his last opinions. He would search his soul while God stood waiting anxiously, changing weight from one foot to the other. What would he say then? He hadn't prepared his thoughts. He had no words. "I'm sorry," he'd have to tell God. "I'm not afraid."

But God had not rushed up yet.

William Bryce Talbot had come to the mountains thirty-eight years before to look for gold. It had been his dream since childhood, since the Sundays in Ohio when his grandfather called him to his cane chair and said, "Billy Bryce, do you know what this is?"

"I know," he said.

"Take a good look now. Go on, so you'll know it."

William Bryce's grandfather held his open hand a little higher than eye level so William Bryce couldn't see into it. A white linen handkerchief was draped over the hand. He stood on his tiptoes, and when he did that his grandfather raised his hand, dangling the white edges of the handkerchief.

His father nearby lowered the newspaper he was reading. "Why do you do that to the boy?"

"Do what?"

"Tempt him. Billy Bryce is going to work for a living. He's going to be someone."

"I hope so," his grandfather said. "I'd like to see money made in this family one way or another."

Then he lowered his hand and removed the handkerchief, and William Bryce saw what he already knew was there: a piece of dull rock.

"Know what that is?" his grandfather said.

"Gold," said William Bryce.

His grandfather died when Billy Bryce was nine, and his

memory of the day was seeing his parents' friends around the casket in the parlor. Billy Bryce had gone upstairs to his grandfather's room and searched the top drawer among all the white handkerchiefs, but the gold wasn't there.

When he was eighteen, William Bryce went to Cleveland. He'd been apprenticed in an upholstery shop. For days and weeks he repaired sofas, recovered chairs, caned chair seats. He was good at measuring and quick with tacks and a hammer, and he had a good eye for color. He possessed attributes valuable to the work, and after two years he started his own fabric and upholstery shop in Shaker Heights.

Competition drove him away. Not that he'd failed: he'd succeeded. He'd made enough money to send some home — his father was sick with tuberculosis. But mornings he wakened and looked out of his dim apartment to the faraway smoke in the faint daylight. He imagined how the smoke was fueling the city, or rather, that the city was what was left after the fuel had been burned. He dressed and went off without breakfast to be the first person at work.

In 1950 no one thought of looking for gold anymore. The country was exhausted by its rush to recovery after the war, and the lingering fear of falling back into Depression drove people to seek jobs with security — any job to cling to like a life ring. William Bryce was part of the recovery: he knew his talents. He prospered from others' success: as people got more money, they bought more fabric, fixed up their homes, purchased settees, screens, canopies. Among all the fabrics that passed through his hands, the one he remembered most clearly was his grandfather's white linen handkerchief.

His mother lived with his sister's family; his father had died. He had never married, never spent money on himself. When he sold the business, people were surprised. What would he do? Wasn't he afraid, not having work? Surely he needed to plan for the future.

William Bryce had planned for the future: he disappeared.

For a long time William Bryce had wandered in the mountains picking up stones, examining them, throwing them down. He was not looking for gold, exactly, though of course he was, but instead for something to attach himself to. He asked himself questions he couldn't answer: what was he doing this for on his few days away from the business? He liked the warm baths, which was how he had decided to vacation there, but he never went to the spa. Instead he roamed the hills, hiked the canyons, teetered on granite ridges and looked out at the sky. At night, by himself in his hotel, he felt the loneliness anyone feels who has given himself time to think.

The next year he came again, free of the business. He built a shelter of poles and canvas among the spruce trees on a parcel of wilderness, moved the shelter from stream to stream, as if on whim. He spent his days exploring, walking, talking to himself, digging in the earth in one place and then another. He imagined the rock his grandfather had revealed to him in the handkerchief as clearly as the first day he'd seen it: greenish, no sparkle to it, but heavy. He'd held it in his hand. That dull rock was an emblem.

In town they laughed at him. The shopkeepers treated him with the disdain they showed to most visitors or to oddities — witty remarks struck behind his back. They possessed the nervous fear people had around anyone unpredictable. When they saw him on the sidewalk, they gathered around him and asked questions. Had he found what he was looking for? How long was he going to go without a stop at the barber shop? Wasn't it cold up in the mountains? They were glad to sell him whatever he had money to pay for — a horse, beans, nails, a rifle, stove pipe, cans of food. They watched him walk out of town again, and they shook their heads in wonder.

He built a wooden sluice of logs he trimmed himself, washed tons of gravel in the rushing water. Evenings he hiked back to his shelter, sat on a bench outside, tired, contented with what he had done that day, though he had nothing to show, no reason to feel satisfied. No one else was there.

Over the years, he had less and less to do with the town, and he ceased to be a curiosity. The jokes and questions diminished. He rarely answered questions anyway, so fewer people asked. He

paid for his supplies as always, loaded them onto his horse, walked
the horse up the highway, and returned to the mountains. People
left him alone.

The early morning light slanted through the window onto
his chair and table. William Bryce raised himself to one elbow and
felt the pain. "Which only proves I am alive," he said.

He poured himself a shot of whiskey he kept for occasions as
he dictated them. It burned in his empty stomach.

With effort, he got up from the mattress and kindled a fire
in the barrel stove, then went outside to the spring. Never in all
the years he'd lived in the mountains had the spring ceased to flow
from the earth. And the water was pure. He dipped the bucket
and washed his face and drank from the ground.

His relatives came to mind, and he imagined the stories they
told about him, the legends they had made up to explain his dis-
appearance — that he had run off with a woman, or had sailed to
Asia, or maybe that he'd headed south to Mexico to live on the
beach. He had believed someday he would go back to Ohio and
make peace with whoever was left in his family: he wondered how
his mother had died, what the news was of his sister and her children; who had married whom; who had been born.

Those were his times of misgiving. Home lingered in a
man's heart when he left it behind. And yet he was glad to be
where he was. The longer he stayed away, the more imperceptible
time had become. Days went by with the water in the streams,
with the melting snow and the rains, with the weathering sun.
Seasons turned past his doorway. One thing he knew: he had not
wasted his life. He had proof of it.

But he had not gone home, and now he was in too much
pain. Proof. He looked across the valleys rimmed with light. There
had been too many mornings he had watched that sunline move
along the flank of the mountain. There had been so many miles of
breaking trails through brush, over logs, into steep ravines, and
many hours of coming to conclusions. He had spent enough
nights alone to cure himself of phantoms.

He turned from the spring. Frost was still on the roof of the
cabin, still on the bench in the shadowed doorway. He carried the
bucket inside and poured water into a pan and put the pan on the

barrel stove. He threw in two more sticks of wood, and the room swelled with heat. He found his dirty clothes, ached dressing himself, set about making coffee. He poured whiskey into the coffee and took the steaming cup outside.

The sun cleared the trees. The heat from the stove inside melted the frost from the roof. The land stretched around him — the valleys, the solid force of foothills laced with scrub oak and spruce, the distant shimmering peaks. He finished his coffee, fetched his rifle from the cabin, and went out to the corral and shot his horse.

He had never kept accurate track of time, but he knew it was the beginning of the pain of many days. In the city the world was a distant place, apart from himself, a false lender. The city kept his mind occupied with glittering images: plays, movies, restaurants, baseball, politics. But it withered his soul.

In the mountains, there was no distance except through air. He rested in the natural changes. Where he lived, it was not death that troubled him, or God's potential questioning, but what would go beyond his death into a world in which he had lived so well.

He leaned the rifle against the door and lifted from the floor his canvas knapsack which he had readied the night before. He buckled the pack closed, slung it over his shoulder. Then he returned to the sunlight.

For the first few hundred yards he went by the way he had worn the trail. But soon after, he diverged from the path and walked cross-country. The mountain was bathed in light. He crossed a stream and angled upward along the slope. He had worked all the creeks and knew them as he knew his own body — each cascade, each rill, each pool was a feeling he kept in himself. In every season, he knew the water and how it flowed. He knew the sun and the angles it cast, the shadows of trees and rock outcroppings, the places along the ridges where the sun rose and disappeared.

He climbed over fallen timber, broke through brush streaked with sun. The twigs and branches snapped against him. He struggled up the crest of the granite ridge and down into the next valley. The pain did not stop. He did not expect it to. It consumed him as time consumed the days. Each day he would be able to do less and less, each day he would grow weaker, and so he was beginning at the farthest stream. Each succeeding day he would have to climb a shorter distance from the cabin. That was how he had chosen it.

He remembered a day years before — how many years he didn't know — when he had tumbled down into a brown meadow. It was in the time of early melt when only a few patches of grass were opened to the sun. There were no flowers. He had cried out his own name and laughed and spread his arms wide, seeing suddenly all around him, in the jumble of bushes and leafless aspens and matted grass, an absolute order. Every drop of water the sun melted moved downhill. Every drop trickled into a rivulet or sank into the earth or rose into the air. Nothing — no blade of grass, no animal, no flower — could live without dying.

In the early afternoon, William Bryce Talbot stopped beside a stream and lay his canvas pack on the ground. He was tired, and for a long time he watched the water flowing past. It had its own source high above him in the snowfields, its own way. It changed even in a single day according to the temperature of the air, or the precipitation, but it continued.

Always there was the pain, but it was nothing to fear. He bent over the stream and tried to see himself in a pool. But though it looked still, the water was a moving surface. His image was fragmented in the swirl. He got to his knees beside the pool, but saw nothing clearly.

Then he opened his pack and thrust his hand into the gold dust and drew out a fistful of it. It was heavy as the rock in his grandfather's handkerchief. And he had more: more in the pack, more in the cabin. He opened his hand in the sunlight and smiled. Then he lowered his hand into the icy stream. The water took it, pulled the gold from his hand and back to itself. ▲▲▲

Wind
Shift

"You've been standing there too long," the old man said. "You're making me nervous." He spat into the dish beside his chair and looked at Glenn.

Glenn was at the screen door. A half dozen cowboy hats lined the rack on the wall beside him, but Glenn wore a blue Kawasaki cap. He was thin, angular, dressed in jeans and a long-sleeved green-and-black plaid shirt. He didn't turn toward his father, but rather spoke into the screen, looking out into the yard. "He went to see her," Glenn said. "You know it, and I know it."

"He's up on the line, sure as hell's coming, and it damn well is. He wouldn't do that other now."

"Clark would do anything he damn-well wanted," Glenn said.

The old man pulled the blankets higher over his legs and turned on the radio again. The stations from Montrose had bad static, and he snapped the radio off. "You'd think there'd be news," the old man said.

"You don't need news," Glenn said. "Look out the window."

Glenn had watched through the screen door off and on for an hour, and each time he looked out, the red half-circle glowed brighter above the spruce trees beyond the ridge up toward Dexter Creek. Dexter Creek was where his father thought his brother was, where the fire surged and receded like wisps of northern lights.

Now and then a bright spark shot up like a meteor into the gray-red sky, but the fire wasn't close enough yet for them to see flames.

"You remember that time in the Weminuche when lightning touched off that windfall?"

"I was three," Glenn said. "I don't remember when I was three."

"It was down along the Animas River," the old man said. "We had to pack in there an hour just to get to the flames."

"I've heard the story," Glenn said. "Maybe ten times."

"Why don't you come over here and play cribbage?" the old man said. "Clark will be here when he gets here."

Glenn turned from the door and looked into the living room. The old man's gooseneck lamp curved over the table where the deck of cards and cribbage board sat on a loose pile of hunting and fishing magazines.

The doctor had said the old man was going to die, which was why Glenn had come home. After the stroke, the old man's hair had turned white overnight, the way a night of deep frost killed the meadow grass, and he'd grown thinner, but he hadn't died. Natural stubbornness had kept him going for the difficult three weeks Glenn had been home. Glenn hadn't seen much change. The old man's moods were still nasty. He bitched all the time, told the same stories, and ordered everyone around.

"I don't want to play cribbage," Glenn said.

"Then go out and check the horses," the old man said.

Glenn didn't move. Through the screen door, the meadow and the line of trees beyond had faded into darkness, and the white gate down the driveway was gray now, a ghostly pale lattice. He wasn't looking for Clark's red pickup anymore. Instead, he expected headlights to appear, high beams shining into the trees and then down through the thin smoke into the yard.

Ellen Jeffries had moved to the Uncompahgre Valley when Glenn was sixteen, which was the first winter he'd started serious work. He wanted to buy a motorcycle so he'd hired on at the Jeffries Ranch. Ellen was twenty-four and married, a slim woman, five feet four, with brown hair cut short like a man's, and eyes so sure they seemed to look right to the center of what she wanted. She was as tough as she was pretty, and Glenn liked her right away.

But he hadn't cared for Craig Jeffries. Craig was a drinker, twice as old as Glenn, and abusive to Ellen. Every afternoon when Glenn rode the school bus past the Silver Eagle Saloon, he looked to see whether Craig Jeffries' truck was parked out front. If it was not, he knew when he got to work the hours would drag past, heavy as bales of hay; if it was, he was glad because he had Ellen alone to work the chores with.

The Jeffrieses had one hundred and twenty acres of hay meadow in the valley, some timber on the ridge, and a small herd of Herefords he fed in pens. Glenn mixed the ration, ran the feeder truck, and cleaned manure from the lots. He irrigated and repaired fence, and during haying season, he worked extra on the windrower and baler.

In winter he cut and sawed timber for their wood stove and doctored cattle, a sideline he'd learned from reading about it. His gift had always been getting along with animals. He sweet-talked the cattle into taking injections without putting them into a nose clamp, and the animals in sick bay recovered faster than if a vet came on rounds. Once Ellen fetched him to look at a cow calving in the barn, and he'd saved the calf from suffocating in its mother's womb.

"I heard the way you sang to her," Ellen said. "That's why she let you get close to her."

"You think so?" he said.

"Why don't you sing to me?"

He smiled, but didn't say anything. He could never have sung to her.

"What have you decided about college?" she asked. "We have to plan for the fall."

"I'm thinking," he said.

"I can get you a raise," she said, "if that'll help you stay on."

Before he'd saved the cow and calf, Ellen had never paid much attention to him. He wasn't particularly good-looking: red hair that made him feel like a freak, and he wasn't strong or very quick on his feet. He quit basketball to make the payments on his bike, partly because of the bike, and partly because he wasn't the shooter Clark was. Besides, ranch work suited him, and he liked being around Ellen.

One evening that spring, a strange thing happened. Jeffries hauled cattle to Grand Junction to sell and hadn't shown up back at home when he was supposed to. It was payday, and Glenn stayed toward dusk, waiting for his money. To kill time, he loaded manure into the pickup and spread it on the garden. He was up in the bed shoveling, when Ellen appeared at the back gate. She had on a white blouse almost luminescent in the dark.

"My husband called," she said. "He's in jail in Grand Junction and won't be back till tomorrow."

Glenn stopped shoveling and leaned on the shovel.

"I know you'd rather have cash," she said, "but I can write you a check."

"A check's all right. I'll finish this."

"Leave it," she said. "It's too dark."

He pitched the shovel into the pile of manure. "I have to look in on the calf in the sick bay," he said.

The sick bay was off in the trees behind the barn and toward the river, and they walked together, saying nothing. He was surprised she came along, but he was glad. An owl called from the cottonwoods beyond the house, and a bright planet shone above the trees. Then she took his arm like a lady taking a gentleman's at a dance, and she pressed close to him. She'd never touched him before.

They stopped at the side door of the bay. "You'll be gentle, won't you, Glenn?" she asked.

He was so surprised he didn't answer. His first thought was he smelled like manure. But at least he had the presence of mind to open the door for her.

"Over there," she said. She led him by the hand to an empty stall, and they knelt in the dry hay.

It was his first time, and she had to lead him. He was thrilled and happy, and blind as the nameless planet he had seen minutes before orbiting along the stars.

His father's guess about Clark's whereabouts was the usual

implied criticism: Clark was up the Dexter Creek Road on the fireline doing the responsible thing, while Glenn was selfishly wasting time. Early on, they'd all had the same expectation, that Glenn and Clark would take over the guide business. Clark was the people person: he talked up the trips, got people to pay, sat with his father and the clients around the cook fire at night and told stories. Glenn was the one who cared for the pack horses — fed them, shod them, doctored them. He named them all after Western-movie heroes. In the fall, he led the pack animals up the Horsethief Trail and set up the camp, and when the camp broke, he brought them home again. It was an old and complex arrangement Glenn had never understood or felt used to — Clark the basketball star, the college graduate, and Glenn the ranch hand, ready to be in business together when their father quit.

And then Glenn had vanished.

He'd been gone for two years. Two years. But when the old man had the stroke, Clark knew where to call him. "Come home," Clark had said. "He's not going to last long." The only way Clark had known where he was was from Ellen.

His father scanned the radio dial again, as impatiently as before, swearing as voices came and went through the static. Glenn crossed the room to the rifle cabinet, opened the glass, and took out his father's handmade 30-30.

"What are you going to do with that?"

"Check the horses." Glenn put some shells into the pocket of his windbreaker, then flipped the bolt and looked through the empty chamber, down the smooth, silvery-gray tunnel, lightly oiled. He snapped the bolt closed and aimed the rifle out the window, looking through the scope across the yard at the chrome of his motorcycle that caught the smoky moonlight.

He'd been taught to feel nothing when the animal was hit. Squeeze the trigger gently and see whether the animal moved. If it jumped or lurched, it was dead. If it didn't fall and didn't run, keep calm, keep the animal in the scope, and shoot again. The old man had taught both his sons this, but only Clark had learned it right. Clark was the hunter, Glenn, the bleeding heart.

Glenn lowered the rifle from the window and looked at his father. Ironically, he was the one who physically resembled the old man — the same thin build, the reddish hair, the deepset blue eyes. But in temperament, he was like his mother. He couldn't remember much about her except she liked to ride Tom Mix, and she liked to stand in the meadow and look at Mount Sneffels and Whitehouse Mountain, as if — and this he'd imagined — she were thinking of another life somewhere. He was like her. He felt her softness in his bones.

The static of the radio drew him back to the room. "You're dreaming again," his father said.

"I was thinking about my mother."

"Don't."

"How do you stop thinking?" Glenn asked.

He left the old man and went out into the yard. He couldn't see the horses, but down in the pasture he heard them pawing the ground, snorting, rattling the rails of the corral. A hint of smoke drifted in the air, and he knew the horses smelled it ten times stronger than he did.

He looked in the window briefly at his father fumbling with the radio dial. The old man leaned closer, shook the plastic box, and glared at it. That was the way his father treated everyone around him.

Then, as his father twisted the radio in the air, a clear station came in. Glenn heard muted words through the window, though he couldn't make them out. His father looked around the empty room. "Glenn! Hey, Glenn! Goddamn it, where are you?"

Glenn turned away from the window and walked down the grassy slope toward the corral.

Like his mother, Glenn understood the need to run. But he hadn't run from the absence of love, the way his mother ran from his father, but rather because of it. He'd loved Ellen Jeffries. She was married, lonely maybe, but married, and what could she see in him? He was a boy.

Oh yes, it had happened. They'd made love. They'd spent that spring and early summer waiting for their chances. When Jeffries was there, heat lightning flashed between them from a distance, and when he wasn't there, they'd tumble into love wherever they found a place — on the seat of the tractor, in the pasture, against a wall in the sick bay — anywhere except a bed. They couldn't wait. Glenn was scared by the fury of their bodies and by Ellen's certain claim he was what she wanted.

One free afternoon he was headed home to a meeting with his father, Clark, and a client who wanted to go into the Big Blue Wilderness to hunt bear. Glenn was late, and he cut the bike loose on the straightaway by the cemetery, ran the canyon like a madman, and cruised the stretch of road by the Timberline Texaco. On the last curve into town, he saw Jeffries's truck parked at the swimming pool.

Ellen leaped to his mind: she'd be alone. He imagined her naked down in the cottonwoods by the river, her head thrown back, and a smile on her face. He forgot his meeting. He turned the bike around and fired back down the canyon. He thought of nothing except pure motion, the kaleidoscope of light and dark, the splashes of sunlight on the road.

He slid into the ranch yard, shut off the bike in front of the house, wheeled his leg up over the saddle. "Ellen?" he called. "Ellen!" He got off the bike and unbuckled his belt to tease her.

Then Craig Jeffries came out the door onto the porch.

Glenn coaxed the motorcycle through strange cities like Fort Worth (one month), Shreveport (five months), Alexandria (two months), Natchez. No one would think to look for him in the South. No one wanted to find him anyway.

He thought after a few months he wouldn't think of her anymore, and without him she'd patch things up with Craig. Maybe she had, but the months didn't help him forget. He took odd jobs. The heat in the South was new. So were the trees dripping with moss, water everywhere, the scent of flowers and salt instead of sage and spruce. The hot days scorched an outline around his life: he found other rhythms and learned the hard, unfamiliar pain of being in places he didn't know.

In Natchez he loaded freight on barges — six in the morning till four in the afternoon. After work he shot pool and drank beer with the men on his shift, then went back to his rented trailer to sleep in the air-conditioning. That was his life's circle.

He met a dark-eyed black woman named Janine, the sister of

a man he knew on the dock. She came to his trailer and drank beer and watched him with languid, sidelong glances while he stripped down his dirty jeans and pulled his sweaty T-shirt over his head.

"You have red hair even on your arms and legs," she said. She rolled the cool amber beer bottle across her forehead.

"Lots of people have red hair," he said.

"Such white skin. No marks at all." She set the bottle down and unbuttoned her blouse halfway down to show him how different her skin was from his. She had a scar above her breast. He touched the scar, then ran a circle around it with his fingers.

"What are you really doing in Natchez?" she asked.

"Working."

She unbuttoned her blouse the rest of the way and smiled at him. "You don't tell me much, honey, but you don't have to say it in words."

"Meaning what?"

"There's a woman in this somewhere."

He took her wrist, backed her against the wall, and held his body against her so tightly she couldn't move. "There's no woman," he said.

She fought him half-heartedly. "Do it hard," she said. "I want you to show me you can."

Afterward, when Janine was gone, he got drunk and wrote Ellen a letter. He was sorry he was such a poor liar, he wrote. His father and Clark invented tales of living through avalanches, killing bull elk with pistols, rains lasting twenty days. In the guide business, people wanted to hear stories. He knew her husband had wanted to hear a story, too — how Glenn had come back to check on a bloated steer or to look for something he'd lost. But he couldn't lie. He could think only of what was true. He loved her. The most he could do was be silent, and in his silence he'd told the truth.

He had no choice but to leave the valley. The Uncompahgre, the San Juans, Colorado were names to think about from a distance. He hadn't forgotten her.

When he finished the letter, he walked a block to the mailbox and put the letter in.

Time went on. Natchez became familiar. Janine came and went. The details of his days were like learning a language by watching and listening. He came to like the slow river and the way the dark water drifted. The heat and humid air became part of him. He liked Janine and the distance between them. She made no demands. Work never ended.

He had got used to Natchez and liked it, and then Clark had called him to come home.

The horse corral was down a grassy slope two hundred yards from the house. Glenn made out the shape of the railing, the horses clustered together at the gate. He whistled to them as he approached so they knew who it was, and they quieted down.

In his absence, some of the horses had been given away or sold because they couldn't pull their weight on the trail. "They cost money to feed," his father said. "I dumped Bob Steele on a family in Colona and sold Tonto and Cassidy to the riding stable. They were no use to us."

"But they were good horses. They did the work all those years."

"Clark shot Gabby Hayes," his father said. "You think we owed them something?"

"Yes."

"Where were you if you cared so much?"

Glenn leaned the rifle against the rail and climbed up onto the lowest board. Mack Brown came over and nuzzled him, and Glenn put his arms around the horse's head. Glenn had never thought of the horses as pack animals, never as plodding or dull. "It's all right," he whispered to Mack. "You'll be fine. Hold on now."

Clark had bought a half dozen new horses Glenn didn't know, and they stayed apart from him, but Mack Brown and Dale Evans and Tom Mix came around.

Tom Mix was his mother's horse, old now. Dale Evans nudged Mack away and let Glenn stroke her nose. Tom Mix stayed aloof. But they were all skittish from the smoke.

Glenn sang them a version of Willie Nelson's "Angel Flying Too Close to the Ground."

If you had not fallen, I would not have found you
Angel flying too close to the ground
I patched up your broken wings, and hung around a while
Trying to keep your spirits up and your fever down...

As he sang, he remembered the snowy day he had watched
his mother ride Tom Mix across the meadow and up the long hill
at the back of the pasture. That memory was true, without words
to distort it. She had faded behind the gauze curtain of snow and
disappeared and never came back. They'd found Tom Mix three
miles away, tied to a tree by the county road. Footsteps in the
snow. Tire tracks. She was gone.

The wind came around to the north, and new smoke slid
along the downslope and through the trees. Glenn stopped singing
and climbed down. "I've got to go," he said. "I'll be back."

He left the rifle there and walked up toward the house.

His father snapped on the porch light. "Glenn, Goddamnit,
where the hell are you?"

His father turned the light off and on again, off and on.

Glenn met his father at the door.

"They're making a stand against the fire at Dexter Creek,"
his father said. "They need every available man."

"Did they say Clark was leading the charge?"

"Don't be a smartass."

Glenn helped his father inside and got him settled back in
his chair by the radio.

"You could go on up," his father said.

"And I should leave you?"

The old man looked at him with an expression of contempt.

Then suddenly there was a different eerie whine to the wind.
It made the wires to the house vibrate and it moaned under the
eaves.

"Wind's changed," Glenn said.

The old man nodded. "Shifted north."

"The fire's going to run past Dexter Creek like a freight
train."

Glenn went to the screen door again. It was black outside
now, the moon covered with smoke. The yard was hot with fire.

"You should go see about Clark," his father said. "Get up on the fire line."

"He's at Ellen's."

The old man fiddled again with the radio. "What if he is?" he said. "She needs someone."

"What do you know about need?" Glenn asked.

His father turned up the radio, but there was more static than voice.

Then he yanked the radio from the wall, and at the silence, Glenn turned toward the room.

"Someone had to be nice to her," his father said. "That was not a crime. You left her. You left her to get beaten up by Craig Jeffries."

Glenn had not gone to see Ellen when he'd come back from Natchez. Clark said she had moved to a cabin up in Elk Meadows and was working in the Outlaw Restaurant in Ouray. She was doing okay. It wasn't a time for romance. The old man was in the hospital then, just about dead, and who knew what would happen? Anyway, he didn't know how to say what he felt. Talking about his feelings was something he'd never learned. It wasn't like doctoring cattle you could learn by reading in a book. He knew he loved her, but that was all, and he couldn't say that.

Besides, they'd had to take up the slack for his father in the business. There were letters to write, horses to work in, firewood to cut for the camp. Two weeks went by, three. Janine and the slow days on the river melted away. It was as if he hadn't left. The old smells of hay and pine and horse manure, the sweet dry air — everything was the same.

But the old man hadn't died. He got stronger and angrier. The doctors kicked him out of the hospital for swearing at the nurses, and Glenn and Clark brought him home.

A few days later, Ellen phoned. "Clark told me you were back," she said. "How's your father?"

"A bastard, as always," Glenn said, glancing at his father by the window. He carried the phone into the kitchen and looked out at the meadow.

"Who is it?" his father asked. "Goddamnit, who're you telling I'm a bastard to?"

"It's been a long time, Glenn," Ellen said. "It seems like a long time."

"Is it Ellen?" his father asked. "Tell her to come see me."

"How are you?" Glenn asked. The meadow swam in his eyes, green against the darker spruce and pine beyond it.

"Didn't Clark tell you?" Ellen said. "We're getting married."

That was how Glenn found out.

Headlights scattered across the windowpanes, and Clark's truck kicked up dust along the driveway. Two high beams riffled through the smoke in the meadow and intensified as they drew nearer. Clark swung the truck into the yard and let the engine die, though he left the headlights funneling out through the smoke toward the corral.

Glenn opened the screen and came out. The door fell to behind him before he realized Ellen was in the cab.

Clark opened the driver's door and got out. "Dad all right?" he asked.

Glenn didn't answer.

"We lost the fire at Dexter Creek," Clark said. "The wind's behind it now. We better hurry."

Clark came around through the headlights, and Glenn saw his shirt was black with soot, and torn. His face was smudged with char, and he smelled of smoke.

"Damn it, move," Clark said. He pushed past Glenn into the house.

But Glenn didn't move. He gazed at Ellen in the cab, then feeling the need to do something, moved off along the edge of the headlights toward the corral.

The smoke was thicker down the hill. He leaned against the corral gate where the headlights didn't reach, but he could see back to the house where Clark and Ellen were carrying out boxes and suitcases to the truck. They would tell stories — how the fire had dried up Dexter Creek, maybe, how they'd come back in the nick of time to save the old man from the flames. They'd barely made it down the driveway as the fire swept through the meadow.

In the corral, the horses pawed the ground and whinnied and danced. Glenn tried to calm them by singing, but the noise of the wind erased his songs. The sky surged red and darkened again. Every few minutes sparks burst above the trees.

A low muffled roar began, carried toward him from an unknown distance like a dream. He knew what it was. Fire on the wind. Glenn felt as if he was on his motorcycle hurtling through the canyon, faster and faster, without steering.

Then Clark came out of the house and down the slope a little way. He stood in the headlights between Glenn and the house. "We're ready to get Dad out," he called. "They've set up an evacuation station at the school."

Glenn opened the gate of the corral, and a half dozen horses galloped past him into the yard, raising dust, running madly toward the trees. The others stayed in the corral, panicked.

"What the hell are you doing?" Clark said.

"I'm helping," Glenn said. "What's it look like?"

"You're scaring the shit out of them." Clark shielded his eyes with his hands and watched the horses scatter into the meadow. "We're all packed, Glenn. We're ready to go."

"I'm not ready yet," Glenn said.

The wind slacked a moment, and the sky beyond the trees swelled yellow-red. Glenn picked up the rifle from where he'd leaned it against the corral. Two more horses galloped out of the corral, but not Tom Mix and Mack Brown. They came to the railing where Glenn was.

Glenn raised the rifle, aimed past Clark, and squeezed off a shot. The right headlight on the truck shattered, and its smoky light faded into darkness.

"It's the light that scares them," Glenn said.

Smoke swirled through the solitary headlight of the truck. Several horses ran back and forth through the smoke like ghosts of horses.

Clark turned and headed back to the house. Ellen came outside, and she and Clark exchanged some words. Then Ellen came down the slope and into the lone headlight.

"Glenn?"

"Right here."

He went into the corral and slapped Dale Evans on the flank, and she and Mack Brown ran out together through the gate and disappeared into the meadow. Their hoofbeats moved away. Tom Mix didn't budge.

Ellen walked to the periphery of the light. "Come and talk to us, Glenn."

"Come and talk to me," Glenn said.

"Glenn!" His father's voice came from the doorway of the house.

"You shut up," Glenn shouted. "Hear me? You keep your fucking mouth shut."

Glenn rested the rifle on the top rail, aimed at the porch light above the door, and broke it with the touch of a finger.

Clark came down the hill toward the corral. "This isn't the time to talk," Clark said. "We need to get out of here."

"Ellen's staying with me," Glenn said.

He came out of the corral and moved off toward the meadow. A wild yellowish light from the fire burst above the trees.

"The hell she is," Clark said.

"I'm not going to hurt her," Glenn said.

"Goddamnit, Glenn," his father called. "Get up here."

"It's all right," Ellen said. "I'll stay if that's what Glenn wants." She looked over at Clark. "You go ahead and get your father into the truck."

Clark went back up the hill, and Glenn watched him carry the old man to the truck and lift him into the front seat. Glenn shouldered the rifle and focused on his father. In the scope his father's face was haggard . His father mouthed some words and looked toward Ellen, and Clark answered and looked toward Ellen, too, and then closed the door.

Glenn lowered the rifle.

Clark went around the front of the truck through the lone headlight and got into the cab. Glenn couldn't hear the truck start. The wind was howling. But the truck moved forward, its headlight jerking over the ground. The light swung around toward Ellen, feathering through smoke, and the truck picked up speed. Suddenly Glenn saw what was happening. Ellen had moved off into the dark, and as the truck got nearer, it slowed, and she climbed up into the bed and ducked down. The truck accelerated, fishtailed, and raced away.

Glenn lifted the rifle to his shoulder and aimed at his father's head silhouetted in the headlight as the truck moved away. Glenn had been taught to feel nothing. But it was a lesson Glenn had never learned. He lowered the rifle.

The red tail lights of the truck receded down the driveway and passed through the murky white gate. The smoke covered the lights before they went into the trees.

Glenn sat on the top board of the corral, holding Tom Mix around the neck. The flames were visible now above the trees and illuminated the house and the corral and the meadow. "A half mile," Glenn said. "Maybe less. Should I tell you a story?"

Tom Mix was calm as long as Glenn was holding him.

"I don't know any stories. I only know what I have to do."

He let go of Tom Mix's neck and climbed down from the railing. "I have to go away again," he said. "I have to go away."

He picked up the rifle and moved off from the corral and up the hill to the motorcycle. He stopped there and looked around. The house and the corral and the meadow were eerie in the jagged firelight, the shadows moving, the colors — green mostly — fading and becoming brighter as the flames surged and diminished. Glenn lifted the rifle and aimed at Tom Mix. Squeeze the trigger gently and if the animal jumped or lurched, it was dead. He squeezed the trigger, and Tom Mix jerked suddenly, as if the noise of the shot had frightened him. He went down on his forelegs, and blood came up to his mouth. Glenn flung the rifle away as far as he could into the grass.

Then he swung himself into the saddle of the bike, kick-started the engine, and eased the bike forward. He drove down the hill and cut through the meadow and rode up into the trees on the same trail his mother had used years before. ▲▲▲

Encounters

Avis was paying for the super-unleaded with her Mastercard when she saw the man. He was young, twenty-four or so, with unfashionably long sideburns that made him appear slightly unkempt. He wasn't so handsome, really, but he had the most perfectly-shaped jaw and chin she'd ever seen — curved like sculpted glass. And deepset eyes. And it was odd that even as he surveyed the magazines on the rack, he seemed to know he was being watched.

Her first thought, realizing this, was she could stare as much as she wanted to because she'd never see him again. Besides, her husband Fred was in the Stuckey's connected to the station, stand-ing behind two overweight teenaged girls. He was oblivious to her. Fred stared up at the black corrugated plastic sign with white interchangeable letters spelling out the menu — hmburgr, cheez melt, chkn salad — as if he were lost.

Avis's second thought was she shouldn't have worn shorts.

That was silly. She'd put on shorts that morning because the forecast was for hot and more hot, and driving through Kansas she'd wanted to be comfortable. She was thirty-eight, and who else but Fred would see her? But now suddenly she was self-con-scious. Her knees bulged, and her ankles felt heavy.

The man was dressed casually but well, in a dark blue short-sleeved shirt and beige slacks. He had delicate hands, slender hips, a flat stomach. He thumbed through *Auto Week*, slipped it back onto the rack, then moved down the aisle toward the cold drink dispenser. She was certain she'd seen the man before, but where? Maybe on television. He might have been on one of the soaps, though she hadn't kept up with soaps for some time. Or maybe she'd seen him at the state realtors' convention. But that was in Colorado. Besides, she'd have remembered. She watched surreptitiously as he pulled a Dr Pepper from the cooler.

"He's pretty, honey," the woman at the cash register said, "but you still have to sign the receipt."

"Oh, I'm sorry." Avis scribbled her name hurriedly and pushed the paper across the counter.

The man came up the aisle to pay for the Dr Pepper, glanced at her, and smiled briefly in a way that didn't let on whether or not he saw her.

Avis turned and went outside to wait for Fred.

They had just left off their daughter, Gretchen, at a Young Episcopalians' camp in Wichita, and had stopped for gas in Garden City on their way home to Durango, Colorado. Fred had driven all the way so far, but now Avis was going to take a turn, so she got into the driver's seat and sat sideways with the door open. It was nearly a hundred degrees, and no moving air came through the car.

Still, the shorts bothered her, and she reached into the backseat and got a sweater to cover her knees.

Fred came out with two vanilla soft-ice-cream cones wrapped in napkins. The man with the Dr Pepper held the door open for him. The two men walked side-by-side for several paces, then diverged, Fred coming toward the Buick, and the other man — he moved so gracefully — striding toward a Nissan Pathfinder at the next pump. The Pathfinder had Wyoming license plates.

For the next week, back in Durango, Avis thought of the man repeatedly. She remembered exactly his expressions, what his hands looked like, the ambiguous way he smiled at her. She didn't know a soul in Wyoming, but of course it might not have been his car. Or he might have lived somewhere else and kept a car at his ranch. She had a persistent urge to take a few days off from the real estate agency where she worked and drive back to the gas station in Garden City to ask the clerk whether she remembered the man. Had he paid with a credit card that had his name on it? If she knew his name, maybe she could find his address. But instead she enrolled in an aerobics class at the fitness center.

"You?" Fred asked. "What for?"

"To look better."

"You look fine," he said. "Why do you want to look better?"

She stared at Fred and didn't answer.

Aerobics classes were Mondays, Wednesdays, and Fridays.

Gretchen came home in mid-August and brought with her a friend she'd made at camp, a girl from Lenexa, Kansas, whose parents were in Europe until the end of the month. Natalie was Gretchen's age, fourteen, and had short brown hair and a bow mouth and, compared to Gretchen, was slight — only about eighty pounds. Avis was sure she had seen Natalie before.

"You look so familiar," she said, "but you weren't in Gretchen's cabin."

"No," Natalie said. "I didn't even get to the camp until the week after Gretchen."

"You couldn't have seen her," Gretchen said. "Remember, you talked to her mother?"

"Of course I remember," Avis said. "Are you a gymnast? You look so limber."

"I'm just me," Natalie said.

Once, passing Gretchen's room, Avis had looked in on the girls as they were getting into their bathing suits to go to the swimming pool. Natalie had her back turned and was stepping into a blue suit. Her body was so thin it had no waist, and when she stood in profile and pulled the straps up, Avis saw she had only wisps of breasts, barely differentiated, even in silhouette, from the rest of her body. Gretchen beside her seemed enormous.

Avis felt old. Thirty-eight wasn't so old, but age was more emotion than a specific number of years. She slipped past the room and leaned against the wall near the window at the end of the hall and looked at her reflection. There were wrinkles around her eyes and the deepening lines on her forehead made her vow not to raise her eyebrows. That's how wrinkles formed. And at aerobics, she must stop grimacing. She passed her hand into the window's light. Her skin was leathery, and blue veins jutted along the tendons to her fingers.

For the rest of Natalie's visit, Avis was barely civil to the girls. She refused to let them take the horseback ride, or walk around the college, or go to the Centennial mall, or even rent a movie.

"What's wrong with you?" Fred asked.

"Nothing is wrong."

"Gretchen says you're not being yourself."

Avis didn't know what that meant — being herself. She bought skin lotions and creams which she applied three times a day to her hands and face. She went shopping and added yellows and pinks to her wardrobe, along with four pairs of brightly-colored shoes. She got a permanent so her hair was as curly as that of the women in magazines.

Finally Natalie's parents picked her up on September first, and after that Avis used lotions only at night, and she let her hair straighten out.

Just before school started, Avis showed houses to a woman she was certain she'd seen before. The client's name was Patricia Sorensen, a tall blond, nearly six feet, with a model's face (though her figure was too sturdy). She had high cheekbones, and her long hair was arranged on top of her head in an elaborate coil. Even the woman's name was familiar: Patricia Sorensen. Avis repeated it to herself several times to see whether it struck a chord. Maybe she had seen the woman on the social page of *The Denver Post* or on a poster somewhere. TV came to mind. Was she a weather forecaster? Had she been on a talk show? The woman didn't say much about herself. She was from Phoenix, and Avis gathered she wanted to move to a cooler climate. Avis didn't know a soul in Phoenix.

The woman judged each house Avis showed as if by a single glance, and Avis felt her sales pitch was irrelevant. "The ceilings in this dining room are twelve feet high, and in the early morning the sun pours in. Well, not exactly. After ten o'clock it pours in.

Look at the view of the red sandstone cliffs!" The woman never asked about taxes or the school or the cost of heating. Apparently money was not an issue if she liked what she saw.

On the way from a house on 4th Street to one north of town, Avis gleaned the woman had just been divorced and had a son who was going to live with the father. That was all. Avis couldn't figure out what, if any, connection she had with Patricia Sorensen. At the house — a cabin, really, though recently remodeled and repriced — the woman treated Avis as if she were only someone with a key to let her in.

It was an eerie sensation to be suddenly invisible. Avis walked through the rooms speaking the words she was supposed to speak, but her voice went nowhere, made no echo, vanished into the clean light that cascaded down from the skylight onto the polished spruce floors.

This feeling of not-being lasted for several weeks. She had felt it before in the Safeway or at the mall, or when she was in Denver to visit her sister, but now she felt it at home and at work where she knew people intimately. How could anyone, this age of computers, satellites, and television, be completely overlooked?

Gretchen, of course, knew she was there. They shopped for clothes and last-minute school supplies; they chatted. And Fred was aware of her. He ate the dinners she cooked, slept in the same bed. But at the same time, he was aware of something amiss. He was more attentive than usual. He touched her cheek at odd moments, kissed her when she was doing the dishes, and held her more tightly in bed. And at the office she wouldn't have said anyone ignored her. Other associates met with her about their listings, wrote her memos, and so forth. But she still felt no one was inside her empty shell.

The weekend after school started, she and Fred and Gretchen drove to Fred's parents' farm over past Cortez. They made the trip every fall for his mother's birthday, only about fifty miles, leaving on a Friday and returning Sunday night, though this year on Friday morning, Avis had closed on the cabin, sold to a Denver doctor for $186,000.

As always when a house closed, she felt as though the sun had doubled its volume of light, and as they drove along the highway toward Mancos the alfalfa fields were such a bright green, and the sandstone cliffs so red, she was certain her perception had been altered by a drug. The crops were mostly harvested then, and the farmers had put on the tables of people across the country a splendid feast of corn, beans, pears, peaches. Even the hay bales that dotted the fields seemed to her excessively neat, almost immaculate in that vivid light.

Gretchen jabbered about her camp and her school buddies, some of whom she was bosom friends with, having known them all of one week. Fred, who was driving, made jokes about the President, and instructed Gretchen not to repeat them to his parents when they arrived.

Then, past Mancos, the countryside turned drier, and they rode in an eerie silence. Avis thought about how the profusion of the fields compared to the arid, rocky hills of piñon and juniper.

Suddenly Avis asked, "Why don't we suffer?"

"We do suffer," Fred said. "We have a Republican in the White House."

"You know what I mean. Like the people in Africa. Why don't we have diseases? And the famine in Pakistan. Why does fate dictate that some people go hungry?"

"It's not fate, Mom," Gretchen said, "it's God."

"Oh," Avis said.

She listened to Fred's explanation about world finances, priorities of governments, how the people themselves caused their own misery by cutting down too many trees, plowing up ground that wasn't arable, polluting their water sources. They drove through Cortez, past the gas stations and Burger King, the Wal-Mart, the Safeway store.

Avis stopped listening to Fred. She thought of the money Fred earned as an electrical contractor and of the money she'd made that morning — six percent of the sales price split with the listing broker — $5,580. She'd make other commissions on other houses. When Fred's parents died, he'd inherit the farm, and when her mother died, Avis would have half of a big house in Boulder, plus her share of her father's trust.

They were never likely to suffer.

In the morning, at the farm, Avis woke early when Gretchen thumped downstairs to do the chores with her grandfather. The screen door opened and closed, and Avis heard voices and the engine of the four-wheeler whir and catch. Suddenly Avis thought something terrible would happen to Gretchen, her only child — an accident — perhaps not then, but later, although at that moment, it seemed imminent. Or Gretchen would have a drug problem, a dreadful disease, paralysis. At the same time, Avis knew nothing like that would happen.

Fred stirred and got up to help his mother start breakfast as he did every year on her birthday. But Avis lay in bed. She dozed and dreamed of a life she might have led in another century, before automobiles and television, before fad magazines and news hype, before absurd encounters with people she didn't know. She and Fred would have lived in such a place as his parents' farmhouse on a piece of land where the seasons would have passed among friends. They'd have needed one another as the crops needed the earth, as the ancient cottonwoods down at the creek needed water. She imagined herself an old woman, gnarled and limping, but calm in a way she knew she would never be.

She dreamed this, and woke to the smell of baking bread drifting up through the floorboards of their attic room like a voice, and the muffled conversation in the kitchen came to her in words disembodied — all the secrets and lies of health and good fortune and prosperity. She heard the high-pitched tone of her mother-in-law's admonitions to Fred and his weak defenses. Then, far out in the yard, she heard the four-wheeler stop. Avis sat up and opened her eyes. After a moment Gretchen shouted to her grandfather about some bird she had seen with yellow on it, and a dark vee on its throat. Her voice was happy, Avis thought, and blind, ignorant forever of the future. ▲▲▲

Light and Rain

Chaney neared the edge of the ridge and looked back down the valley to the north toward Log Hill Mesa and the Uncompahgre Plateau. It was light now, and the sun was pushing the shadow quickly down the flank of the mountain into the Blue Lakes Basin. He watched the jagged intersection of pink and black, and shivered in the cold. They had started from Willow Swamp before dark so they could be secure in the good weather of the morning. It was still too early for clouds.

Briggs was already into the trees along the creek bottom, and Chaney was left behind with Maria. He had followed her for most of the first hour they'd been on the trail, watching her strong, effortless pace. She floated as she walked, her long legs gliding through the dark spaces of the trees and across the dew-wet meadows. For a long time, the red kerchief was the only visible part of her, but as the light seeped into the day, she had taken form: the black pants, the pack, the dark hair streaming under the red kerchief and down her back.

> *She had eyes like Sarjeli's, that same darkness. But Maria's eyes were never quiet, while Sarjeli's were like still water. Sarjeli's eyes pulled you down. Maria's pushed you away.*

Chaney called out, "Elk," and she stopped and turned back. He could tell she hadn't heard what he'd said because she wasn't looking where he was pointing — up the hillside into spruce.

"What do you see?" she asked.

The elk were obscured by the trees and far away. Why should he share them with her?

He didn't understand why Briggs had brought her along. Before, there had been the easy companionship between the two of them — he'd never have had to point out elk to Briggs. Not that he had anything particular against Maria, but he'd thought he and Briggs had an understanding. Chaney wanted to measure his own life against Briggs's, to see whether, after Sarjeli, he was still sane.

Maria filled his vision, getting larger as she came nearer to him. She took off her pack. She was a handsome woman, tall and lithe. She twisted her dark hair at her shoulder and put an elastic band around it. "The stream," she said. "I couldn't hear you."

"It doesn't matter," he said. "They're gone."

He had not thought of the stream below them in the gorge, had forgotten the sound of it because it had started in the distance some time ago. She was right, though: it was louder now that they had traversed the gorge and had come out above it. Just off the trail, down a hill of paintbrush, the white water rushed over the rocks.

"How far still?" he asked.

"Maybe a couple of hours to the first lake." She wiped her forehead with her kerchief, then folded it and stuffed it into the side pocket of her pack. "If the weather holds, Briggs wants to go farther."

"You and Briggs can go farther."

"You'll make it." She smiled at him.

Her forehead shimmered with sweat; her neck soft with dew. Her hair was wet at her temples and beside her ears.

"I'm not worried about making it," he said.

This was true. He would make it. The mud-clogged boots made his legs ache, but he had put in enough time in the mountains to know what he could do. It was not the distance that bothered him.

Sarjeli believed he was so much stronger than she.
Or did she really believe it? There were so many

kinds of strengths beyond the physical, and many
weaknesses. When they stared at each other, he was
the first to blink or laugh. It was the eyes. She could
hold her eyes in midair and, looking into them, he
was reminded how much of her life had been lived
in the presence of death. She had been raised in
death, but it never occurred to her to put an end to
suffering.

Maria hoisted her pack, and Chaney took a step closer to
help, but then retreated. When they were loading up the sleeping
bags, cooking gear, and food, Maria had made no concessions to
the men's strength or stamina. She carried her own, she said,
though she'd allowed Briggs to carry the tent. She had struggled to
put on her pack before Briggs had lifted it for her, and she'd got
her arms under the straps.

And now: she set the pack on a boulder, sat down under it,
and staggered to her feet. He let her be, thinking how it was not
so easy to equalize lives as carrying the same loads. How many
advantages had she already been given by being beautiful?

"All right?" he asked.

"Sure." And she strode on ahead.

For a few minutes he measured time by the angle the sun
made in the scraggly trees at the edge of timberline. It was eight
o'clock maybe, and they were still in the shadow. Once he got into
the sun, the going would be better.

It had never been a question of language. Sarjeli
was studying at Leeds when he met her. He was
thirty, but his youthful looks disguised his aimless
life. He had ideas, but he was farther than ever
from getting anything started. Part of it was his
insistence on being free. How could you work and be
free at the same time?

"Work is being free," Sarjeli said. "In India the
ones who do not work suffer most."

"It's not the same thing."

"But you are merely starting in a different way."

"I have choice."

"Choice," she said disdainfully. She nodded

*calmly, her eyes that bottomless black he could not
endure. "Choice is what makes you miserable."*

The trail led up a steep pitch and over the patterned gray-and-green apron of the tundra. Briggs said once to take the next step before the first ended, then to lock the knee so the weight of the body rested on bone rather than muscle. It sounded logical, but Chaney could not concentrate. He thought of sweat.

In the old days they never had to hurry. That was the feeling. When they'd lived in the Northeast, they'd done twenty trips together in Vermont and New Hampshire. He remembered one day in Pinkham Notch when they'd done nothing except sit in the high bowl of snow in the hot sun and read. Whatever else was left of the world was gone, and what was still to come was far away. It hadn't mattered that time went by.

Maria. He'd never felt with Briggs the urgency Maria brought with her that morning.

Briggs waited for them on a flat rock overlooking the stream, and Briggs and Chaney had Milky Ways and water. Maria ate her own trail mix and strips of beef jerky and an orange.

After the break, Chaney took the lead. The sun had hit them, and though he was warmer and looser now, he still felt anxious. They were beyond the first lake now and on a much steeper pitch to the second. The trail zigzagged among the rocks and trees. Briggs and Maria were below him on the switchbacks, and there was pressure to maintain the pace. He felt as if they were distance runners waiting for the right moment to make their move to the front.

Eagles. Two dark birds soared above Blue Lakes Pass. Chaney was tired and stopped to watch them soar on the uplift that was invisible along the ridge.

Maria caught up first. "Clouds," she said.

Eagles against clouds. He hadn't noticed the clouds — mere puffs of white. The birds held their wings motionless and still raced across the sky. Clouds: they were banked in behind the peaks — clouds they knew were coming.

"We'll make the second lake," Briggs said, "if we don't stop."

*If she wanted to, Sarjeli could hitch a ride any-
where. She was slender and her face was alive with
shades of blue and tinges of rose. With her looks, she
cut easily through the world's fabric. If anyone got a
glimpse of her face, he stopped. Chaney had.*

*Sometimes she wore sunglasses, which changed
her whole countenance. Then she seemed hard,
steeled by experience. She was elegant, charming,
sure of herself, but cold. He never pictured her in
society, though she had been raised with money.*

*They had spent six months together in Europe.
At first she had not blamed him for wanting to
stretch time. He'd finished school. He wanted to
travel, so they hitched to Africa, at first by boat,
then by plane and bush taxi. Sarjeli did what she
wanted, and he followed.*

Chaney kept his eye out for movements along the trail. It
was barren up high, but there were marmots, pika, ptarmigan
camouflaged so well you might step on one. He liked the sun. He
wanted to let the sun inside his brain and let the heat of it burn
away the debris. He didn't want to think of Sarjeli, or Maria, or of
the things he had wasted. He wanted the pain in his legs to stop.
Each step was bitter, an ache, impossible: everything and nothing.

The sound of rushing water faded. The stream from the second lake to the first was smaller and riffled gently over the stones.
Chaney noticed it when Briggs waited for him on an outcropping
where the trail cut to the right. Maria went on ahead.

"You hanging in there?" Briggs asked.

Then Chaney heard the wind. The rush of the wind had
replaced the rush of water.

"Sure," Chaney said.

"You lose your breath when you go soft."

"Going soft wasn't intentional."

Briggs smiled, but the smile was an accusation. "Of course it
was, living that good life in Europe."

"We all changed," Chaney said.

"Have I?"

"You've become more serious," Chaney said.

"We get older," Briggs said. "It's hard to believe, but we do."

"I didn't say anything was wrong with it."

"Neither did I. I wouldn't have brought Maria otherwise. You know that. I don't get to see her much as it is."

"She embarrasses me," Chaney said. "She's so strong."

"We better get after her," Briggs said. "I'll go ahead and get the tent up before it rains."

"How much farther?"

"Not that far. Over this ridge and up another rise. From there you can see the second lake."

Briggs moved forward up the steep slope, and for a few minutes Chaney tried to keep up. But he couldn't hold the pace. His legs gave way under him. He slowed, breathless at that altitude.

Maria was assigned to watch him: that's how it appeared to Chaney. She and Briggs must have had a conversation when Briggs had caught up to her. Watch Chaney, he'd said. He's in trouble. He'd cripple in to the campsite where Briggs would already have the tent set up and the fire going. He didn't like the idea of being left behind with a babysitter.

She was waiting for him where the trail lipped out over what he knew was a false ridge. Maybe she felt sorry for him. She knew he was out of shape, and she was sympathetic. Or maybe she was tiring, too.

He paused a moment to catch his breath and glanced at the sky. The sun had gone under, and gray clouds had built a fortress against the blue. Fortresses and castles: that was how he imagined clouds as a child. Lightning and thunder were attacks by mythical forces.

Maria was waiting for him. and he was compelled to climb higher.

> *They were lying on the bed after making love, her head resting upon his shoulder. Sarjeli said, "You would make a terrible prisoner of war."*
>
> *"I hope I never have the chance."*
>
> *"You would crack within an hour."*
>
> *"Why do you say that?"*
>
> *"Because you're so serious."*
>
> *He'd smiled, but had not understood. "Serious?"*

"I know you love me," she said.

"I don't try to hide it. Why would I?" He did love her. He loved her shyness, the way she refused to let him see her naked. They had traveled together three weeks before she consented to sleep with him.

Then the depth of her need surprised him. She dared him to make love to her in public places. At times he felt more her accomplice than her lover. She wore skirts, no underwear. They'd hurry. And then when they took their time, the thrill was gone.

"You love me too much," she said.

"It's not possible to love too much. It's a contradiction in terms."

"Why is it?"

"Do I love you more than you love me?"

She turned away. "You have led me out of my childhood," she said. "I know that."

Briggs had no notion of fatigue. He was a half-mile ahead of them on the next rise and still pushing forward. The worst thing about watching him, Chaney thought, was seeing the distance he, Chaney, had to cover, how far it was and how steep the terrain.

Maria pushed him from behind. Her pace had slowed, but whether it was because she was tired or he was going slower, he didn't know. She still moved effortlessly, while he labored.

It took another forty minutes to reach the second rise where they saw the lake. Chaney let his pack slowly off his shoulders in relief. Below him, another half mile, was the red tent set up beside the gray water, at the edge of a few trees. Briggs was gathering firewood. The smell of rain was strong on the wind.

From the rise, the view back from where they'd come was multi-colored — the dark waves of trees along the flanks of the granite cliffs, the blue foothills and distant mesas, the gray-brown flats and valleys beyond them. The sun was shining there — it must have been fifty miles away — over Montrose and farther north. The sky without distance stretched beyond his vision, and timeless. The colors and shapes — mountains, cliffs, foothills, mesas, valleys — were disguises for what was hidden deeper.

In front of them was the pass. That was for tomorrow, but

Chaney picked up the trail zigzagging up the side of the sheer scree — no trees there. A series of peaks rimmed the basin. There was snow in the crevasses, and at the end of the lake, a snowfield that fell into the water. Clouds drifted quickly over the summits of the peaks and along the vertical granite. Birds he heard in the air were invisible. The wind swirled down against him, cold without the sun.

There was no hurry now because the weather had beaten them. Gray streaks of rain swept over the far side of the lake.

The trip was to have been a moratorium, but the idea was flawed. Already in his life he'd had too many hiatuses, believing free time — doing nothing, being still — would change things. But he went over the past too zealously. Nothing was allowed to heal.

> He'd believed Sarjeli was an answer. He was willing
> to do anything for her. But where was the future?
> He had no plans. He'd promised to return to the
> States and get settled, find work, find himself, and
> then bring her over. Settled where, how? He'd been
> willing to try.

When Maria came up to him, her hair was loose, and she held it back from her face with one hand. "Can you find my kerchief?" she asked. She turned her pack toward him.

He delved into the side pocket, pulled it out for her. "Do you think you can make it?" he asked.

"Me?"

"You look as tired as I feel."

Rain moved across the lake. Briggs ran for the tent with an armload of firewood.

"He'll be dry when we get there," Chaney said.

"Do you envy him that?"

"Yes. Do you?"

"This first rain will go past us," she said. "But look beyond that."

Chaney did not look. He watched her eyes, dark and aware, tired now. He did not want to take his eyes from hers. "I'm sorry you had to stay back with me."

"I didn't have to."

She looked at him with a tenderness he hadn't seen in her before, a sympathy he might have taken either as honest or false. But he couldn't know: he interpreted both ways, always, though he wished he could do otherwise.

Sarjeli's eyes were so black they did not let you fool yourself. Ever.

Maria tied the kerchief over her head. "We'd better get down," she said.

But he didn't move.

"Are you going to stay here?" she asked.

"For a while."

To Sarjeli promises meant nothing. But his promise had been good. He had come home and found a job. It was not a job he wanted for the rest of his life, but it was something, and he had done it for her.

"But did you find yourself?" she asked.

Maria turned and started down toward the tent. He watched her descend into the swale of green tundra where white flowers dotted the meadow. She crossed the low area. How beautiful she was against the dark green and the flowers! Then she passed over the hump of the swale on the other side and disappeared.

Chaney rested a few minutes — he didn't know how long precisely. The rain moved across the lake and slipped from the basin. Where he was, he felt only a few drops. He lay against his backpack and watched the next storm come toward him.

He felt better now, gathered his strength. It was downhill to the lake.

Two years ago everything was beginning. He hadn't met Sarjeli yet: he hoped time would lead him into what he wanted to do. He had to do something. But the something never materialized. Then he'd met Sarjeli, and they'd traveled. He'd fallen in love with her, and he'd promised to love her. Regardless of time.

Then she'd said she couldn't come. She had not said it so dishonestly as that. She'd said, "I'm not coming, Chaney. It's impossible. No one can maintain the pitch of an emotion forever."

The water in the lake was so clear Chaney could see trout ten feet down. He skirted above the lake and toward the flat grassy knoll where the tent was set up. The first rain had passed, and there was a moment of sun. The lake shimmered in diamonds, with the wind stirring the water. But the second rain moved toward them. Down in the basin he couldn't see it coming. It was beyond the peaks. But he believed Maria. Thunder echoed high up from the granite cliffs. The sun would not last.

He left his backpack beside the red tent and walked to the edge of the water. Briggs was gathering more wood. Maria, he assumed, was helping. He didn't see her pack, but she must have put it in the tent. He washed his face, lifting liquid ice with two hands. The sweat melted away. He stood up, face dripping, and stretched his shoulder muscles where the straps of the pack had rubbed his skin. He dried his face on the sleeve of his shirt.

Clouds: as a child he'd made shapes of clouds. A bull, a castle, a fish leaping. But the clouds had no shapes now.

Briggs had laid the fire, but hadn't lighted it. Chaney opened his pack and got out his poncho and the food he meant to cook.

Then Briggs came from the trees with more wood and dumped it down by the ring of stones. "Where's Maria?" he asked.

"I thought she was with you."

"I haven't seen her," Briggs said.

"She was ahead of me. I thought she'd put her pack in the tent."

They looked at one another. Briggs's expression was calm and relaxed. "She knows what she's doing." He knelt and struck a match under the tinder. "We ought to cook what we have before it starts to rain."

Chaney stood by, wondering how Briggs could be so unconcerned. But it was not Chaney's place to interfere. The flames crackled up through the wood, sputtered into what was wet. He took out the small flask from his pack, sat down, and drank off a capful of bourbon. He poured another and handed it to Briggs.

Briggs took it and drank. That was their ritual. They got off into the mountains by themselves and sat and drank and talked and watched the night come down around them. It was their way of getting to what was real.

But now, after Briggs drank, he did not sit down.

"We need more wood," he said. "There's not much up here."

"I'll go," Chaney said.

"I know where I've been." Briggs paused. "I'm sorry if this isn't what you thought."

"Maria doesn't like me much."

"Relax," Briggs said. "You never used to be so wary."

Chaney poured another capful of bourbon, drank it, and stood up. "She wasn't on the trail. Do you think she could be hurt?"

"Why don't you find her?" Briggs said. "If you have something against her, talk it out."

"I don't have anything against her."

"Is it the Indian girl, then?" Briggs couldn't remember her name.

"Sarjeli."

He believed with a touch he could go with her, but the silence between them was deeper than silence alone. He looked at her — those eyes — and sank into them. That was what mattered. Sinking into love.

"I wish I'd known her," Briggs said. "I wish I'd known her to know what to do for you."

Chaney shook his head. "You couldn't help."

"Who else but me?"

Chaney did not answer the question. "I don't want to go over the pass," he said. "Tomorrow I'm going back."

"You've done the hard part," Briggs said. "What's the use in going back?"

"The hard part is just starting."

Thunder boomed behind the mountains, reverberated in the cliffs and across the lake.

Briggs moved away toward the trees, and Chaney was left to watch the rain. Maria knew it would rain.

She hadn't stayed on the trail or he'd have seen her. She might have climbed behind the ridge above the lake and looked down over them. He scanned the ridge, but didn't see her. Or she could have worked her way toward the creek below the lake.

Either way, Chaney had one path, which was worn by fishermen along the shore. He followed it toward the shallow end. A good-sized trout moved leisurely over the rocks.

To the end of the lake was a quarter of a mile — not that far, but he was tired. Several times thunder rolled over him, and he stopped to check the distance of the storm. The mist swirled over the peaks. The gray rock disappeared and emerged again from behind clouds. Lightning flashed down once over the ridge.

At the end of the lake, the outflow meandered a few hundred feet, then dropped precipitously down a falls. Chaney edged down along the game trails to a point where he could see the water falling into a pool. She was there, lying face down on a rock, her arms stretched out over the water, black hair down her back. Naked from the waist up. Unmoving.

His first reaction was physical. His heart pounded. She was dead.

Then she twitched, and her hands and arms shot down into the water. She grappled with something in the pool. Her own body — back, hips, legs — trembling for purchase. Then with both hands she raised the trout, still flapping its tail, and rolled away from the rock.

Chaney leaned back from the edge and hid himself behind a boulder.

She dropped the trout on the grass beside the pool, picked up a rock, and killed it. She had already caught several others that were lying on the grass.

She sat back for a moment. Her arms were red from the cold water. Her bare shoulders slouched forward toward her dark-tipped breasts. She shivered and looked up toward him, focusing probably on the clouds to gauge how much time she had before the rain. She didn't see him. She unlaced her boots and took them off, along with her socks, and then she stood up and unfastened her jeans.

He could not let her know he was there, but now that he knew she was all right, he did not want to deceive her, either. He raised himself from the boulder where he'd hidden and started down the steep incline paralleling the falls. He called to her once — "Maria" — but the falls made too much noise for her to hear.

She peeled down her jeans, stepped out of them, and waded into the pool. Her body was taut and strong, her skin tanned. She took off her kerchief, threw it onto the grass beside the trout, and shook out her hair.

He ran down the meadow, jumping from one grassy hump to another to make himself visible to her. He called to her again, "Maria."

She bent down and put her hands into the water and drew the water up over one shoulder. Then she heard him and looked up.

He stopped halfway down the slope.

She did not turn away or move from the pool. She held his gaze.

He descended more slowly.

She did not move.

Thunder rolled again, and the rain came with it, misty rain first, on the wind. He felt it on his face, but he kept looking at her.

She laughed and shivered.

He reached the bottom of the steep meadow, level with her. He lifted his shirt over his head and dropped it at his feet. He unbuckled his belt and unzipped his jeans. The mountains had disappeared now. Clouds drifted over the top of the waterfall, and the rain came harder.

> *Sarjeli said he was brittle because he could never*
> *last. He had never loved anyone like her. Those eyes.*

But he did not see Sarjeli's eyes now. He waded naked into the pool, and the rain fell over them. ▲▲▲

Perfect Stranger

The frame shimmied over fifty and the tires weren't good, but Martha kept the Volvo at sixty-five all the way across the high dry plateau to Durango. She'd driven full-tilt for three hours, watching the light move from morning to noon across the mesas, the shadows receding as if they were melting under the glare of the sun. At Aztec she'd had a brief longing to stop — the orchards just turning green looked so pure and fresh, and in a small town like that no one would expect anything from her. She'd find a white house by the river, and there'd be no man to disapprove of her doing nothing.

Besides, the mountains to the north unnerved her. She'd grown up in the New Jersey suburbs of Philadelphia, and her family had summered in the Poconos. She liked the smooth arcs of the Eastern hills draped in maples and laurels and ash. They gave her solace. It wasn't until Peter brought her west to Denver that she'd had any idea what real mountains were like. The Front Range was foreboding— all rock and scree and relentless white snow. And so were the Sangre de Cristos east of Santa Fe where they'd finally settled. Peter had taken the job as a real estate analyst. Martha hadn't minded Denver because the mountains were obscured by smog, and the climate was dry. Then Peter wanted to move to Santa Fe. "The air's cleaner, and real estate is booming," he said, "and skiing's right there."

That had been true, but their life together had fallen apart.

She was still not certain what had happened. Over months Peter had turned distant, so of course, being open herself and desiring to know, she'd asked him what was the matter. If there were a problem, address it. She remembered they were standing in the kitchen, the copper pots hanging like gold leaves from the hooks above the counter, the sun slanting in from the Jemez Mountains.

"People grow apart," he said. "After a while, people want change."

"You've had change. Philadelphia, Denver, and Santa Fe."

"You have to take risks," he said.

"Living with you is a risk."

"That's what I'm saying, Martha. You have to find your own way."

"What does that mean?"

"I want a divorce," he said.

It was nearly two-thirty, and already she was cutting it close getting to Gunnison for the party. She'd left a little late from Santa Fe, and now, almost to the Colorado border, she felt the press of time. Lisa had insisted there be a celebration. "A transition requires a ritual," she said. "You put behind you what's gone."

"I've already put it behind me."

"I'll invite some eligible men," Lisa said, "and there'll be plenty of women with divorce stories worse than yours."

"But do I want to know them?" Martha asked.

Lisa laughed. "If someone else's pain is worse than yours, you want to know about it."

The divorce was over now, and she was relieved. At least she thought she was. The lawyers had steeled a compromise on the real property, and she and Peter had parceled out their possessions according to the principle of most involvement: she got the books and records; he took the VCR and the television. She had even met his new friend, Ynez, who seemed jittery and much younger than he was. She was dark-haired, pretty, a good athlete, and Martha could see why Peter would be glad to find Ynez in his bed.

From Durango the road paralleled a river — cottonwoods

told her where the river ran. The terrain beyond the river was sandstone cliffs, junipers, scrub oak, and higher up, pine and spruce. Far in the distance was a panorama of jagged peaks with snow.

There was only one highway north. The map said Silverton, Ouray, Montrose.

In the foothills, the Volvo labored, and a Jeep Cherokee pressed on her tail. Ahead, a silver semi-trailer truck was even slower than she. She braked and measured the Jeep in her rearview mirror. The husband and wife were arguing. The woman yelled and waved her hand, and the husband yelled back, though Martha couldn't hear anything. Martha thought the man was going to pass, but a blue sedan came from the other direction.

The semi shifted down, and as it slowed, it revealed, behind the cargo carrier, a blond young man at the side of the road with his thumb out. He wore a blue jacket and carried a sign. That was as much as Martha saw.

The road cleared in front of the truck, and she passed, accelerating through the shimmy to sixty. In her rearview, behind the truck, the Jeep Cherokee swerved into the turnout where the hitchhiker was standing.

It was foolish to pick up anyone these days. The young man was probably a college student on his way home for spring break, but there were enough horror stories about hitchhikers to give them all a bad name. Of course the door swung both ways. Plenty of maniac drivers cruised for victims to rape and murder. The truck was in a swale behind her, and she saw in her rearview the hitchhiker running awkwardly toward the Jeep with his backpack and his sign.

Years ago — so many now it was hard to believe — she'd hitched a few times herself. Her parents had forbidden it, naturally, and the officials at the high school warned all the students not to do it, so there was a natural temptation to go for the cheap thrill. Usually she thumbed with other students downtown or out to the mall in Cherry Hill, but now and then she took a ride alone. She'd hitched once to New York up the Jersey Turnpike. One driver, she remembered, talked her ear off. And a woman who picked her up at Exit 10 confessed her husband wore women's lingerie. In the Lincoln Tunnel, another driver agonized about his children's hating him. On the way back that same afternoon, she'd got a ride from a man who asked her questions: how old are you, sweetheart? What's your name? What are you studying in school? She never thought much about his motives. Then a couple of weeks later, riding from Haddonfield to Collingswood, a man picked her up who hadn't said anything. He was young and well-dressed, short haircut. They'd driven several miles without a word, and he'd seemed variously curious, bewildered, and, to judge from his silence, angry. When they got into Collingswood, she told him where to let her out. She could walk to her friend's house. "All right," he said, "if you'll show me your breasts."

At the next red light, she'd jumped from the car, and as soon as she was clear, he'd gunned through the intersection. Probably he was as afraid as she was. But it made her wonder: was that what men thought about?

The high peaks disappeared behind the nearer terrain of sandstone and scrub oak. The Volvo climbed past the Tamarron Resort and some isolated ski lodges and into the spruce forest. Each curve gave a new vista of the canyon, a rock face, waterfalls, a snow-covered couloir. That was the way it happened: the clear view of the world changed every day.

The Jeep Cherokee roared by on the long uphill before the summit of Molas Pass. Arizona plates — not the maroon-and-white ones, but the new one with the lilac saguaro. The Jeep zoomed ahead, creating distance and more distance.

Over the years, she and Peter had built up security little by little — a house on Zia Drive on the hill east of Old Santa Fe Trail, some investment property out in El Dorado, a townhouse rental. Mr. and Mrs. Peter Christian. For the first time, Peter mentioned wanting a child.

Then a month later, he was talking about moving to Europe.

"What's wrong with Europe?" he asked.

"Nothing's wrong with Europe."

"Oh, God," she said suddenly, "you're having a mid-life crisis."

They'd been sitting on the terrace looking over the low-slung adobe houses to the west toward the Jemez Mountains. The hills had already sifted toward blue in the late afternoon light.

"It's not a crisis," Peter said. "Don't you want to see new places?"

"And meet new people?"

He'd paused, and in that instant she knew he'd already had an affair.

"No," he said, "not like that. I mean scuba dive in Greece, climb the Eiffel Tower, see Aida in the Baths of Caracalla. I was thinking of taking up hang-gliding."

"Really?" she said.

The chill of Peter's momentary confession lingered. She had never considered herself helpless before. For eight years he'd filled her house and garden, and then in one moment he was saying she was worthless.

But she'd let the incident go, convinced his estrangement was a phase. An affair, like hang-gliding, was a symptom, not a disease.

The top of the Molas Pass was 10,910 feet. Snowfields were alongside the road. Water ran everywhere. All around were mountain peaks. There was a sign about watersheds, and the red Jeep was parked beside it. The couple had got out and were shivering in the cold wind. Martha didn't stop. The peaks and the snowfields and the dark forests with shadows of clouds across them frightened her.

She accelerated on the downslope, then braked because the hill was so steep.

After he'd taken some hang-gliding lessons, Peter wanted to solo, and she'd gone up with him to the Santa Fe Basin to watch him hurl himself into space. He'd run headlong toward the cliff, whooped and yelled with his typical bravado, and dived from the cliff. He soared outward on red and blue and yellow wings like a beautiful parrot.

He even lived to brag about it.

But she knew her own limits. She didn't care about scuba diving or the Eiffel Tower. She'd never have jumped off a mountain with only a few stitched-on colors to keep her afloat. If she had, would he have loved her?

The Jeep appeared again in her rearview mirror and grew larger as it sped toward her. What was the point of doing sixty when there were 25 mile-per-hour switchbacks every half mile? The Jeep pulled out, drew even, and passed in slow motion. The wife was apparently reconciled. She was reading a magazine in the front seat and didn't look up. The hitchhiker sat in back, his head propped in one delicate hand. He had a clean-looking face and a wistful expression, blue eyes.

Lisa said Martha had given up too much in the divorce.

"I don't care," was Martha's answer. "Peter wanted adventure, he gets adventure."

"He also gets Ynez," Lisa said.

Peter hadn't liked Lisa from the beginning, and she hadn't liked him. She was imposing — tall, prematurely gray, a straight-talker — the maverick daughter of family friends, someone Martha had followed from a distance. When they'd moved to Denver, Martha had looked her up one skiing vacation to Crested Butte. Lisa had thought nothing of taking seven years to get through college — jobs, travel, a semester course now and then. She'd worked in an art gallery, quit to write for a magazine, then retired, as she said, to paint.

"She's got no discipline," Peter said. "That's her problem."

"She paints every day."

"She dabbles at fish and bicycles."

"She's good," Martha said. "She does landscapes, birds, flowers. . ."

"Flowers, too? I rest my case."

Lisa's version was different. "He's angry because I didn't light up for the pass he made. What does he expect, every woman to fall for him?"

"You mean he propositioned you?"

"It's surprising men don't shit through their ears," Lisa said.

Martha's attorney agreed with Lisa. "He left you," her attorney said. "You could kill him if you wanted to."

"I want it over with," Martha said.

"In two years, you'll regret it."

"I regret it now," Martha said.

Mr. Lauer leaned forward in his chair. "His name is Christian. Let's make him give. I mean, money's the bottom line."

"Are you my lawyer or my psychiatrist, Mr. Lauer? What's the use of money if you suffered terribly in other ways?"

Mr. Lauer sighed. "It's your call," he said. "What do you want to do about your name?"

"I want to be myself," she said.

The hitchhiker stood at the highway intersection outside Silverton where U.S. 550 turned north to Ouray. Martha recognized his pale blue windbreaker and the white sign. He raised the sign toward her: GRAND JUNCTION. Honey light from the west shone in his face.

Presumably, because he was standing there, he hadn't robbed the couple in the Jeep. He hadn't killed them. And at that altitude, in the shadow, it was cold. His gaze followed her as she made the turn.

Peter would have been furious if he'd known she even considered stopping. The thought of Peter's controlling what she did made her brake the car and pull to the side of the road. She was stunned how quickly she'd stopped.

She was still well past the hitchhiker. It wasn't smart to pick him up; she knew that. But the man had already shouldered his pack and was running along the highway. Was she committed? No, but Peter loomed up again, and she snapped the car into reverse and backed up along the fringe of the roadway.

The man opened the rear door first, cleared away a couple of shoe boxes, and slid his backpack in. "Thanks a lot," the man said.

Martha collected the litter of maps and tapes from the front seat to make space. "I'm going as far as Montrose," Martha said. "That'll help you some."

"You bet," he said. "Hot dog."

The "hot dog" made her feel better right away. Criminals didn't say hot dog.

The man opened the passenger door and ducked to get in. He was out of breath from running with his pack. As soon as he closed the door, she accelerated, made certain the road was clear, and pulled back onto the highway.

He was younger than she'd imagined — maybe twenty. His hair was long and ragged, but clean, and it hung over the collar of his jacket. His eyes looked tired. If she had one overall impression, it was that he was exhausted.

"Where're you from?" she asked.

"Today from Las Cruces, New Mexico," he said.

"Where do you live, I mean."

"Well, in Eagle Lake. I used to live there anyway. I've been on the road three days."

"Eagle Lake. Where is that?"

"Texas. Near Houston. Not too near, though. More like country. I'm going up to Grand Junction to visit my sister."

The Volvo thumped as it got up to forty. "This car won't move like your last ride," she said.

"I'd rather have a long ride than a dozen short ones," the man said. "That other guy was only going to Silverton."

"His wife was mad at him."

"I guess." The man smiled. He had a good smile, like a slap on the back. "What about you?" he asked. "You got New Mexico plates and all this gear."

"Clothes and shoes. I'm going to a party in Gunnison." She listened to the tick-tick of the tires. Peter had told her months ago to get new tires on the car, but she never thought of it except when she was driving fast. "A divorce party."

"My sister's been married for seven years," the man said. "Nobody thought it'd last, but she just had her second baby. It's my first trip up north. It's pretty, except for the mine tailings."

She looked out the window at the orange mine refuse that bled down the hillside. The divorce party went right past him. She thought of the tires again and held the wheel tightly against a blowout.

The divorce had been final three days before, and up to the end she'd suffered. It wasn't that there was anything to do. The arrangements had been agreed upon. She'd known it was going to happen. But it was like waiting for someone to die — the long slow breathing, the anonymity, the last heartbeat.

When her father was failing, she'd sat by his bed for weeks, watching his sallow, sunken face, listening to his raspy voice. She held his cold hand and remembered the way he'd held her when she'd lost her first dog, how he'd looked at her wedding, the way he'd lifted his chin when he stood at the tiller of the Windsong in the afternoon light as he motored into the harbor at Tom's River. She couldn't hurry him. That was how the divorce was. She'd loved Peter. He was hard-working, intense, hard-playing. They were different, like skiing — she had a natural rhythm, floated down the hill in wide, graceful arcs, while Peter fought the mountain as if it were a dragon to be slain. Once in mid-summer, he'd run naked into an icy lake above Aspen. Once he'd made love to her in an elevator. A hundred images filled those days of waiting — what he'd looked like walking into the living room, the set of his jaw when he got stubborn, the way he looked at her when they made love. He was dead now, but not dead. He was with Ynez.

The road climbed quickly, paralleling a creek with willows, and then leveled off in a glade of pines and spruces. Above the trees, the hillsides were steep and green and rocky, much more forbidding than New Mexico. The hitchhiker stared out the side window as if following every nuance of the landscape.

But his eyes drifted closed.

"You can sleep if you want to," she said.

"I hate to sleep when it's so beautiful."

"I can wake you in Ouray. I thought we'd stop for gas and something to eat."

"I'm a little tired," he said.

He wriggled out of his windbreaker, wedged it against the side window, and rested his head on the jacket. He slept the moment he closed his eyes. Even sitting up, his whole body relaxed. His mouth yielded its tight expression, and his eyelids twitched. His hands, uncallused and miraculously clean for someone on the road three days, lay open, the thin fingers curled slightly inward on his lap. She noticed these things because they slowed so much for the hills. She felt guilty for looking at him, as if she were violating a confidence. His mouth was open, and his breath seemed to come from somewhere deeper than his lungs, from some great dark place where words were born.

A pickup honked behind her. In her absorption in the profane act of watching, she had slowed down to twenty, and the truck had closed on her. The driver pulled out to pass, and the man behind the wheel gave her the finger. That was the kind of intimidation Peter practiced. When she got tired skiing, he got impatient, and when she kept on and fell, he was angry at her for holding him up. Or he might criticize her for not saying what she thought at a party, and when she spoke up, he'd laugh at what she said. She gave the pickup driver the finger back, though he was already well ahead of her.

The hitchhiker shifted his position and sighed, and his left hand fell from his lap into the space between the seats. She wanted him to talk. He was tired, but he might tell her something about his life. What did he mean he used to live in Eagle Lake? And why did people think his sister's marriage wouldn't last? If he had been on the road three days, how was he so clean? His face was clean-shaven. In the angle of the light, the distinct line where the razor crossed his cheek looked so severe. His blond hair, obviously washed, shone bright yellow. Was it the light that made him look so gentle, or was it sleep? His hands were delicate and smooth, and the wisps of hair on the backs of them looked soft as feathers, and she had an impulse to touch his fingers just to feel how soft his hands were. But what if he weren't asleep? If a perfect stranger touched her that way, she'd have been outraged.

Mountains loomed up around her — high rocky cliffs, snow in crevasses and on corniced ledges of granite. She was petrified driving Red Mountain Pass.

When Peter had first driven her around the West, he'd pointed out mountains he wanted to climb — Pike's Peak, Mount Elbert, Crestone Needle — but she could not imagine anyone brave enough to set foot on them. He was brave, Peter was. She had to give him credit for that. He was brave to ask for the divorce.

Martha was braver than Peter. That's what Lisa said. She'd called frequently during the months before the divorce. "I know what you're going through," she said. "I went through it twice myself."

"But you were glad of it."

"The important thing is to plan the future. Go out with other people. Show Peter you aren't afraid."

"I don't want to go out."

"He's in pain," Lisa said. "He's not a happy man."

"How can he be in pain? He does what he wants. He has money, energy..."

"Gerbils have energy, but they live in cages and go around on wheels."

"Peter doesn't live in a cage."

"Of course he does."

Martha kept thinking of the flowers Lisa painted — irises so blue they were like ice, and poppies red as dawn. Her studies of motion were beyond Kepler — a brook trout rising in dense water, a gold Schwinn bicycle being repaired upside down with one wheel spinning. What Lisa lacked, she thought, was not discipline, as Peter had said, but warmth.

On the right, a cliff knife-edged straight to the pavement, and on the left was nothing — a dropoff of five hundred feet. She crept past two markers for people killed in avalanches, edged past Bear Creek Falls, and coasted the straightaway. In the distance the yellow-lit valley and mesas of the lowlands beckoned her.

When she struck level ground in Ouray, she veered to the side of the main street and stopped. She was shaking. The hitchhiker opened his eyes. "You all right?" he asked.

"I wanted a hamburger," Martha said, "but that restaurant looks all right." She pointed to the lighted sign across the street — The Bon Ton. "Are you in a hurry?"

"It'll be dark when I get there either way," he said. "What about your party?"

"I don't care. It's not important," she said. "I'll be late."

"You have to eat," he said.

The restaurant was fancier than she'd imagined from the outside — a dimly-lit bar and tables with white tablecloths. A well-dressed hostess led them to a table.

"Would you like something to drink?" the hostess asked.

"Just water," Martha said.

"A beer for me," the hitchhiker said. "Budweiser is okay."

The waitress nodded and pulled out the chair for Martha. "I'll use the restroom first."

"Upstairs and to the right," the hostess said. She turned and pointed.

The hitchhiker sat down and picked up the menu.

"Get whatever you want," Martha said. "I'll pay."

The man looked up and smiled. "Fine with me," he said. "You bet."

In the bathroom she combed her hair. God, why had she had it fluffed like that? It was a hopeless brown mop. She put on a touch of lipstick. She had pretty skin. Peter had always said that, and nice eyes, and good breasts. She tucked in her blouse, the back of which was damp from sitting so long in the car, and looked at her profile. She did have good breasts — ample and upright.

Then she pulled her blouse out and went back into the toilet stall. She took off the blouse and her bra, stuffed the bra into her purse, and put the blouse on again.

She came out and looked at herself again in the mirror. The print fabric still masked her breasts, but the effect was clear. That's what men thought about. She leaned in toward the mirror, smiled at herself, and wiped a smudge of lipstick from the corner of her mouth.

The man stood up when she came back to the table, and he stared at her as she sat down.

Their conversation during dinner was pleasant enough. She asked about his family. His father ran a farm and a feedlot. His younger brother, who played high school basketball, helped with the chores. He himself had repaired televisions and VCR's at a shop in downtown Eagle Lake. His one sister, the one in Grand Junction, had married a fruit grower.

"What's it like in Eagle Lake?" she asked.

"Like nothing."

"You sit around and listen to the crickets?"

"Geese," he said. "Eagle Lake is the goose capital of the world."

She laughed, and he smiled the slap-on-the-back smile.

"Really," he said. "In winter there are geese everywhere — Canadas, White-fronts, Snow Geese. Mostly Snow Geese. Thousands of them, hundreds of thousands."

"Do you shoot them?"

"Some people do, but not me."

He was silent then.

"So you're on vacation now?" she asked finally.

"Well, sort of. I got fired from my job."

"And do you have a name?" she asked.

"Taylor Lanier," he said.

"Taylor Lanier. I'm Martha."

"Martha what?"

"Martha Lynn Gray."

After dinner he went to the bathroom, and she paid the check. She put her credit card back into her billfold and looked at her makeup in the mirror on the flap of her purse.

"Ma'am?"

Martha looked up.

The waitress was holding out to her Taylor's blue jacket. "Your boyfriend wouldn't want to forget this," she said.

"What? Oh." Martha closed her purse and took the jacket. Heat seeped into her face.

Outside the sky over the mountains had faded to an eerie blue without stars. Where the sun had gone down, a blend of orange and blue and pale white outlined the dark forests and the paler mountains. Lights shone dimly down the main street.

"Thanks a lot for the meal," he said.

Walking to the car, she carried his jacket over her shoulder. She wanted to take his arm with her free hand, but she couldn't bring herself to it.

"How far to Montrose?" he asked.

"About forty miles." They paused at the passenger door, and she unlocked it. "Do you want to drive?" she asked.

"I'm pretty tired still," he said. "Unless you want me to."

She lingered at the door. She felt he ought to drive if only to thank her for the dinner. But she felt more he ought to kiss her.

He smiled at her, then opened the door and slid into the seat.

She threw his jacket in after him. "You left this," she said. "If you haven't got any money, you should be careful about your things."

Headlights across the median drifted in and out of her awareness. The Volvo slid past the town swimming pool as if on oil. Vapor rose into the air. The eerie colors ebbed from the mountains, and north of town, darkness settled in. They rode past the cemetery.

"What was it like getting fired?" she asked.

"Ma'am?"

"You said you got fired," she said. "Were you ashamed?"

"I never thought of it that way."

"How did you think of it?"

He paused, and she looked at him. Apparently he hadn't heard her cold tone because he was thinking.

"I was making good money," he said, "but I was sitting, you know? I was just as glad to get out."

Her headlights sprayed across the asphalt, along the pasture fences and weeds. The land sloped upward on her right. Isolated arc lights of houses shone from the river bottom on the left, and then a mile or two farther on the lights of another town gathered. He was quiet again.

"What'd you get fired for?" she asked.

"They said I was lazy 'cause I'd take off work and ride my bike out to the sloughs. I'd sit on the levee above where they'd come in from feeding, and pretty soon I'd hear them honking, and that kind of soft evening light filled up with geese — geese everywhere — the darker Canadas and White-fronts, and thousands of Snow Geese. They'd crisscross and make patterns like in a kaleidoscope, and then they'd swoop down and settle on the water. It was a once-in-a-lifetime sight, and I saw it every afternoon."

"They fired you for that?"

"Yeah, for watching the geese."

He was quiet again, and she looked at him. He smiled briefly, and in the darkness she couldn't see him well, but she thought the smile was more to himself than to her. He was thinking of the vision of the geese, same as she was, and the quiet made her feel helpless. When he didn't speak, she was invisible.

But why should he care how she felt? He was just a rider in her car.

And lucky. If he could repair TVs and VCRs he could get work anywhere. She was giving him a good ride to Montrose. A week at his sister's in Grand Junction, and he'd light out for California. He'd get up one morning and walk outside and hold out his sign. That's what being a man was all about.

She signaled right and veered off onto the shoulder. The man grabbed for the dash.

The car stopped.

"Get out," she said. "Get out of my car."

He stared at her.

"You heard me. I said get out."

He gazed through the windshield as if confused by the oncoming headlights of another car, by the darkness. Beyond the short grass along the roadside one hill was indistinguishable from another.

"I didn't mean to cause any trouble," he said. He snapped open the door and stirred from the seat.

A cold blast of air filled the car. She was surprised how frigid the wind was. She imagined him standing by the road with his thin jacket on. No one would see him in the dark. Or someone who meant to harm him would stop.

"Wait a minute," she said.

"I'll be fine," he said. He lifted himself from the seat and stood up outside the door.

"I'm sorry."

Sorry. That was how Peter made her feel — as if she'd done something wrong. If he knocked over a glass, it was her fault because she'd left it in the wrong place. If he left her, it was her fault. But now she was sorry.

"Please, get in," she said.

Taylor paused, then got back into the car and closed the door. Heat swelled into the tight space. In a few seconds she was up to speed on the highway.

The man was silent again.

The Volvo shimmied in the darkness. To order him out for no reason and then to invite him back: he must think he'd latched onto a crazy woman. She couldn't stand listening to the tires humming.

"Tell me a story," she said.

"Pardon?"

"A story. Tell me why you're so clean."

"Oh," he said. "That's not a story."

"You had a girlfriend. You stopped in Las Cruces to see a woman."

"No, ma'am. I slept one night in a field, and the next night out behind a truck stop. But this morning — it seems a lot longer ago than that — I was walking out of Las Cruces real early, just barely getting light, and I passed this motel with a swimming pool. Nobody was around so I took myself a bath, and I shaved in a gas station bathroom. I figured if I looked decent I'd get better rides."

His voice faded into the lights of the opposing Texaco and Conoco stations at the intersection of the road to Ridgway. God, she'd have been so afraid to do something like that. But for him it was easy. So what if he got caught? Nothing would happen — no humiliation, no danger. He'd get dressed and go on his way.

They crested the hill beyond Ridgway and slipped back into the night. She kept her eyes straight ahead on the road.

"What are you going to do in Grand Junction?" she asked.

"Stay with my sister."

"I mean, besides that."

"Nothing much. Look around a little."

"What if I gave you money?"

"Money to do what?"

She knew the man was looking at her, but she dared not look back.

"How much would you need?" she asked. "What if I gave you a hundred dollars?"

"Why would you do that?"

"To go with me to the party in Gunnison."

She lifted her purse from the seat, found her billfold, and took out two fifties. She held the bills out into the empty space between them.

"A divorce party," he said. "You the one the party's for?"

She let the bills drop. One floated to the floor beneath his feet, and the other landed in his lap. He picked them up and held them in his hand. She waited for him to say something, for thank you or no thank you, or let's find a motel, or where are you going to let me out? But he didn't say anything.

She drove for minutes, miles. The lights of houses were farther apart. They passed a reservoir, the moonlight shining from the water. The longer the silence lasted, the smaller the car became. They were closer together, but more distant, the way in intimacy lovers became strangers again.

Then the land was flatter, the lights more frequent — ranches, arc lights on garages, houses. Taylor was asleep holding the money. His head rested against the side window, and his eyes were closed. He breathed through his mouth in deep draughts, as if he were speaking to her. Yes, yes, yes, he was saying. She touched his hand, intending to wake him. In daytime Montrose would have been any ordinary small town, but at night it was a galaxy of lights moving as the Volvo moved and vibrated, lights like geese flying in the darkness.

After she touched him, she withdrew her hand. He was tired and needed sleep. Yes, yes. He would sleep another two hours before they reached the place she wanted to take him. ▲▲▲

Toward the Sun

Nieman runs in the mountains. He starts from our small house at 7700 feet, and in a few minutes I see his tattered gray sweat suit drifting among the dark spruce on the Twin Peaks Trail. When I return from the garden with the day's pick of beans, lettuce, and squash — we get no tomatoes at this altitude — he will be coming out of the Oak Creek gorge at 8500 feet. I like to watch him there because the trail skirts through scrub oak and along a cliff, and he is in the open for several minutes until he turns the corner and crosses the meadow into aspens.

I lay the vegetables on the porch step, wipe my hands on my blouse, and pick up the binoculars. In the circle of the glass, Nieman's maroon form is muddled by heat waves from the neighbor's roof, but I do not need perfect focus to be absorbed. Against the red sandstone, he holds his arms perpendicular to his body, as if he were a hawk tilting its wings to catch the thermals and updrafts which swirl among the crags. He reaches out with his long legs and steps lightly over the rocky trail, darting as the path twists along the contour of the cliff.

I know his face, the physical strain in the creases of his eyes and in the tight, pursed lips. His distant expression is somnambulant and dreamlike, though Nieman claims he never dreams. I imagine sweat beading on his forehead, oozing into his eyes, and I recreate his face with the serenity I wish were there. In my leisure, standing by the vegetables, I make him over.

And in Nieman there is much to want to change.

First, I would change the legend. The stories about him are both widespread and exaggerated because he neither confirms nor denies the details. To many, Nieman is heroic, superhuman. When he runs he never tires. When he races, which is seldom now, he wins without apparent effort. His stride is longer, his body in better condition than anyone else's. In high school fifteen years ago, he ran a mile in four minutes flat, but when colleges tried to recruit him, he said he couldn't run on level ground. He stayed in the mountains and went to college nearby so he could run as he wanted.

I know Nieman's unusual power. Once I climbed Mt. Sneffels with friends, from the Blue Lakes side — a seven-mile hike with an elevation gain of almost five thousand feet. We started at eight in the morning, and by three in the afternoon were nearing the summit. Nieman had lunch in town and beat us to the top.

Yet it is not the legend itself that troubles me so much as what it does to Nieman. He does not exactly believe his own press, but the stories have an unsettling effect on him, as if inciting him to further outrages, to harder tasks. To me, his myth is another shadow on a body which already has too many.

When I met Nieman three years ago, I was painting, studying with a man in Santa Fe. I had just begun to discover my own natural affinity for spare colors, for light. I understood space and temporal mood. Perhaps in my personal life I had too much comfort, but I felt strong, and at the time Nieman was on crutches.

"Your fault or his?" I'd asked, nodding at the cast.

"Man versus machine," he said.

He smiled, but his face was sad. His eyes were uneasy, as though there were in them a tautness or impatience between mind and heart.

"I tried to race a car to an intersection, and I thought the driver was playing the game."

"So it was yours?"

"He never saw me," Nieman said.

At the time, of course, I didn't know Nieman was that kind of runner. I assumed he was one of the millions who'd taken to the fad. He was a good-looking man who raced cars to intersections.

I didn't know he was sick.

Sick. Perhaps he's not sick, but fanatic. A zealot without a cause. I can understand the desire to hone the body to a fine edge, to increase the endurance of the muscles, to strive for greater lung capacity. But those motivations are superfluous to Nieman. His body is already beyond fitness, past the limits of endurance. He wants to push away the routine of daily life, to escape. But where? He is in the mountains five or six hours a day. If he could eat and sleep on his feet, he could run forever. No one runs like Nieman simply to take his mind off his problems.

He leaves the cliff edge and climbs to the meadow. His brown hair tufts in the wind, his legs drive effortlessly uphill. His ragged sweatsuit sways and dances against the pale green. He breaks into the clearing and crosses suddenly from the sunlight into the shadow of the dark timber.

Nieman, I know, does not mind the shadow. To him the warmth of the sun and the cold of the shadow are the same.

"Why can't you tell me?" I asked him before he left.

"Tell you what?"

"What you're doing."

He turned away without answer — an admission he is doing something.

He will tell me. He does not keep anything to himself for long, and it is not to lie that he is silent. I cannot accuse him of deception. He has never told me anything false. He is shy and awkward around people, not meant for superficial banter. But he cannot be dishonest. If there were a seed of dishonesty in him, he would, like an oyster, make a pearl of it. That kind of honesty is both hard to come by and hard to endure.

144

Once I asked what he thought about when he ran. When he was in the mountains alone and felt the mist of the clouds on his face, what did he know? When he skipped over roots and rocks and climbed to the ribbons of snow, he must have thought something.

"No," he said. "I don't think about anything."

"Your mind is blank? Absolutely blank?"

"Not blank, but I don't think of anything."

Then he was silent. He smiled at my wanting to know, and I got angry. If he didn't want to talk that was one thing, but to smile as though I were sweet for asking was another. I suppose it angered me that he knew he did not have to explain himself. I loved him anyway. The more he was silent, the more I poured myself into his silence.

He's made me quit painting, though not because he's forbidden it. Nieman hasn't said anything. My vision is not so clear in these mountains as it was in Santa Fe. My sense of color is different; the light is not the same. The rapport among hand, eye, and the land has withered, and I feel stiff and tentative, even when I sketch. I haven't given it up so much as I'm waiting for a time I don't feel rushed.

I don't delude myself. I know the truth is marred by my caring for Nieman. I have given him too much for safekeeping. What troubles me is not that I have stopped painting for the moment, but that in my giving I am still not all Nieman wants or all he needs.

Nieman is a phenomenon as much as a geyser or a meteor. To treat him as normal would be to admit he is the same as everyone else. When he runs beside his friends, it's plain how separate he is. His stride cannot be compared to theirs. His gait has a different energy. To Nieman's one step, the others seem to take two.

Nor does Nieman have the distance runner's lanky frame. His legs are thicker and stronger than the bony-kneed marathon man's. His upper body is slight, but not sunken as those who are all lungs. Nieman is bigger. He has sturdy shoulders and a tapered waist. His arms are long and wiry, and his thighs raw-muscled. He does not tire when he runs. Ever.

Yet he is generous. When other runners seek his advice, Nieman gives his time willingly. He would do anything they asked — lend them money, give his name to causes. Most of all, though, they want to learn how he does it, and he shares with them what they believe are secrets. But his running is not something Nieman has learned and can impart to others. His body is the marvel, and the running is in him alone.

And yet to treat him as extraordinary doesn't help. All it does is give him license to disregard the limitations the rest of us must face. Nieman believes without thinking he can do whatever he wishes. That is another part of him that ought to be changed.

He is gone now from the meadow and has moved into the trees. I pick up the vegetables from the step, survey the carefully weeded garden and the clean wash on the line — everything except Nieman's maroon running clothes. Lately I have adopted his strategy of silence, though it isn't my nature to accept what hurts me. I'm afraid of small things that have meaning. Nieman has let his hair grow. He uses no soap when he showers. He refuses to let me wash his sweat suit or underwear.

And the tenderness in our lovemaking is gone. He holds me fiercely now and presses against me so hard I'm breathless. But in the hurt is a new pleasure: I feel he needs me more.

Do I punish myself? Do I spoil him? Sometimes I want to walk away and give him the freedom to do what he will do without me. But where would I go? I have my garden. The house is now as much mine as his. I'm the one who's expanded the small store from which he used to squeeze out a living. I've brought my brass bed from Santa Fe.

I'm fascinated by the things I know, but he doesn't. I know his body from the outside. Lying on him can be soft, or like lying on marble. He can rock me on his thighs by flexing his legs. My own body gives way. Even now — still — I am surprised how peacefully I sleep against his slow heart.

Nieman says he never dreams, but he wakes in the night running. He babbles in guttural sounds, and he turns toward me with his eyes closed to the moonlight. His body is rigid, and he holds me as though I were a fragile glass figurine. He is dreaming, but when I tell him later what he has done, he says he doesn't remember. He looks away.

I try to talk to him, but he won't listen, or rather, he listens but won't say much in return.

"Are you going to race?" I ask.

"No."

"Travel?"

"You're going with me."

That is all I have.

He runs with such discipline, though he claims it takes no discipline to do what one truly loves. Sometimes when I wait for him at a certain place on a trail, knowing he has to pass me, he surprises me from behind. How does he do this? When the wind is right, he can do the same to a deer. He can run silently and at full speed.

I wonder whether it's I he runs from. I was 26 when I met him; now I'm 29. Nieman is 33. In three years his body hasn't changed except to become stronger. His leg has healed. He has no trace of a scar or a limp. I think about ski racers, about how speed is as much a function of psychology as of physics. Once speed causes pain, the mind forces the body to be cautious. The racer slows after a break. But with Nieman it is the opposite. His broken leg has encouraged him to take further risks.

And yet we age. Nieman ages. He must know his time is getting shorter. I imagine him at forty, at fifty, still running in the mountains, still tireless. I am glad to watch him now, while my painting is gathering strength in me, but I don't want to watch him forever, seeing my own heart move through time and space. I have limits.

He makes an effort for me. He goes to parties because I enjoy other people. We go to movies. Sometimes on weekends he tosses horseshoes at a barbecue or plays softball, though he is no good at catching or throwing. But these parts of his life mean nothing to him, as if, at the same time he is swinging at a softball, he is seeing another, entirely different configuration of forces from the one others see. Nieman's reality is an undercurrent, another time frame, a dreamwork.

Once when we rode home from a party I asked him about the future.

"I don't see a future," he said.

"But we must have something."

"Who?"

"The two of us."

He raised his eyes from the road and turned to me. He didn't understand.

"I don't mean forever," I said, not wanting to offend him, yet offending myself for worrying. "I mean, we should think about what we may miss and can't get back to."

"Regrets," he said.

"Yes. Sometime I would like to..." But the word *child* did not emerge.

The lack of family has something to do with the way Nieman is. He had no antecedents, no parents to look to and see himself. He molds himself to his own image. That's why a child would help him.

I could trick him, of course. Deceiving Nieman would be like deceiving a helpless old man. Nieman would never know. He wouldn't ask whether I meant to get pregnant. If I talked to him openly about our having a child, he'd say no, but if he were confronted with the child's coming, he wouldn't ascribe to me the motive of a lie.

I would be happy if Nieman would change just enough to join my life. He knows I can't wait forever. He can't wait forever. Some say to cage an animal destroys its essence. I have seen a coyote in a zoo pacing back and forth on a sterile concrete floor, gazing through the wire mesh. What kind of animal has it become when it knows it will be fed at intervals, when it is cared for, when it cannot hunt and run free? Is it the same animal I see at the edge of my headlights driving a dark road at night?

If Nieman would change just a little — but then, would he be Nieman?

2.

The air has a nick of autumn on the morning Nieman takes me with him into the mountains. In the high country, the aspens have already edged to yellow. Nieman is unusually quiet. Sometimes when we hike together he speaks of the wildlife or the weather or the history of the mines, but this day he moves quickly along the trail, waiting at intervals for me to catch up. Several times I sense he wants to speak to me. In his face is a strain seldom there. But what he knows he will not tell, and what he will not tell commits us both to silence.

He carries the tent, most of the food, and a thin sleeping bag. I have a lighter pack with a down bag, a pad, aluminum pots which take up space, and paper on which to sketch if the mood strikes me. The trail skirts the wall of a cliff, drops into a stream bed, then rises again into rocky crags. I have been here before: to alpine meadows, steep waves of timber, and up higher to where the trees peter out and cannot grow at all.

Once I stop to rest, and Nieman kisses me and smiles.

"What is it you're going to do?" I ask.

His expression changes. He does not like my directness. Without answering, he starts up again along the trail.

When we reach the end of the second cliff, we move through dark timber for half a mile. Nieman changes again: now he is playful, alert. He acts as though he were leading me through dangerous terrain.

Then finally the high meadows open up before us. The long summer grass has turned dead yellow here, and the hills rise toward benches of yellow-red aspen. Farther away is more dark timber, and above timberline, rocky scree that borders the sky.

Even after we set up our rough camp at the edge of the meadow, Nieman is not at ease. He scans the steep meadows, looking for something, and when I ask what he seeks, he turns away.

That night he makes love to me with a frightening passion, nearly ripping my flesh with his. He does not seem to know me, and I cry out helplessly. Later, when he is quiet, I feel sorry for him, and angry. Why should he torture himself when help is so close by?

In the morning he gets up and wakes himself in the icy stream. He immerses his naked body where I can barely dip my hands. He shouts and splashes and rushes at me laughing, as though to pull me in, but I jump back and run into the meadow.

After breakfast we climb higher. Nieman wears his gray running suit and his running shoes, and he carries nothing. The meadow slopes upward, a steep hill with several glades of aspen. The white bark of the trees is so clean, and a chill comes over me when we enter the halo of yellowing leaves. The trembling heart-shaped leaves make me feel barren.

Nieman stops frequently, still surveying the sides of the valley, still watching the dark timber toward which we climb. Once he pauses abruptly and raises his head.

"What do you see?"

He looks at me strangely, as though caught. "It's what I smell," he says.

I try to catch the scent of whatever it is, but I gather only the aroma of dry grass and a hint of spruce.

We move forward again at a steady pace, but Nieman is now absorbed and deliberate. We pick our way along game trails through another glen of aspen and beyond into a sunny meadow. But even in the warm sun I feel the cool breeze off the mountain, and the day tightens around my heart.

In the meadow we stop for a snack. Nieman barely eats. He stares at the rocky scree and the dark timber above us. Seeing what? Knowing what? He looks old.

Then he nods and utters an eerie cry. I follow his gaze.

Elk. I find them easily in the binoculars. There are perhaps thirty of them, mostly light-rumped cows moving slowly uphill, grazing the shreds of grass which are invisible to me from such a distance. Two spike bulls with dark manes escort the cows.

I glance at Nieman who crouches stock-still.

Then from below the elk, from the dark timber, comes a huge antlered bull. He climbs to the others, stops, and turns his head toward us.

Nieman starts running.

It is astonishing how quickly he moves away from me up the sharp angle of the hill. Within a minute he is into the timber, breaking through brush, leaping fallen logs. I call to him, but he does not hear me, or he hears me and does not answer.

I retreat to the edge of the meadow for a better view, and

Nieman's gray running suit moves among the spruce. He weaves, ducks branches, then stops suddenly in a shaded clearing. In the binoculars I see him bend down and rub his hands in the dirt. He presses his hands to his clothes, then moves to another place near-by and rolls on the ground. He lifts handfuls of dirt and spruce needles and rubs them over his face.

It dawns on me what he is doing. Perhaps I have known before, but I realize it at that moment in my heart: the distraction, the running, the silences. He breaks from the clearing and climbs into the trees. I nearly call to him again, but it would be of no use even were I to scream.

It takes me half an hour to reach the opening in the trees where Nieman's tracks are. I find the markings on the ground where he had gathered the dirt in his hands. I touch the earth to confirm what I know and lift my hands to my nostrils. The smell is everywhere, sickening, so strong it's horror. The odor is of elk urine and the musk of elk beds recently deserted.

From the cover of the trees I can see nothing, so I move higher, aching, knowing how Nieman smells. The game trails are overgrown, and I fight my way through the underbrush. The branches scrape me, catch my anger, but I gain higher ground. Gray granite peaks surround me, and beneath and across stretch the deep valleys where snow lies in perpetual shadow.

I scan the slopes for several minutes before I see the elk again. They have already moved a mile or more into another drainage. The hills dividing each ravine are lines of yellow and gray, one beyond another, sliding downward toward the stream. The elk skirt these hills, running now, sensing the danger behind them.

Then Nieman appears just below the line of the ridge. In the binoculars I see the thin game trail he follows, and as seconds elapse, he becomes clearer. His stride is forceful, strong yet grace-ful. The tension in his face is gone.

The elk cannot see him around the curve of the hill, and he cannot see them. But each knows the other is there. Nieman runs in their tracks. His legs carry him easily, for Nieman never tires. The expression on his face is dreamlike, though Nieman claims he never dreams.

Watching him, I feel a lightness seep into me — weakness and strength. I gaze around: the high country is as foreign as a bleak moon.

The elk run along the base of a huge crag, descend into another valley, then climb higher toward the saddle between two peaks. For a time Nieman closes the gap, but the elk move faster. After a few minutes, they tire, and Nieman gains.

He holds his head straight. His legs reach out, and his arms churn smoothly. I imagine his body beneath the sweatsuit, the sweat mingling with the urine and musk of elk. I wonder whether our child would have Nieman's body, Nieman's elk body, Nieman's resolve.

The elk ascend the last pitch to the saddle, and in the angle of the sun become part light and part silhouette as they disappear over the pass. I shiver and turn away before Nieman reaches the top. ▲▲▲